**Anne Marsh** writes s
paranormal romances
enjoy one more alpha
romance after getting
technical writer—and
ever-afters trumped software manuals. She lives in
Northern California with her family and six cats.

If you liked *Ruled*, why not try

*A Week to be Wild* by JC Harroway
*Off Limits* by Clare Connelly
*Legal Seduction* by Lisa Childs

Discover more at millsandboon.co.uk

# RULED

## ANNE MARSH

**MILLS & BOON**

First Published in Great Britain 2018
by Mills & Boon, an imprint of HarperCollins*Publishers*
1 London Bridge Street, London, SE1 9GF

© 2018 Anne Marsh

ISBN: 978-0-263-93207-2

MIX
Paper from
responsible sources
FSC® C007454

This book is produced from independently certified FSC™ paper
to ensure responsible forest management.
For more information visit www.harpercollins.co.uk/green.

Printed and bound in Spain
by CPI, Barcelona

For Aunt Monica.

For the Monday morning Skype calls, squirrel and slug advice, and the best pictures of a California anemone ever…

Our time together means so much!

Thank you.

# CHAPTER ONE

*Eve*

YOU SEE THAT big pink RV parked next to Lake Mead? That vehicle screams *look at me*. I painted sparkly rainbows and unicorns on both sides, along with my business name. Perfectly Princess Parties. The bling is great advertising, like driving a moving billboard around Las Vegas.

I put the *princess* in *party*—there isn't a five-year-old girl (or boy, frankly) in Vegas who doesn't believe I'm made of awesome. I specialize in birthday parties—we're the precake entertainment. We've got the dresses, the sparkle and the attitude to keep our audience riveted and wanting to be us when they grow up. Eventually, at some point between five and twenty-five, those same girls will realize it takes more than a dress and a crown to rule the universe, but the fantasy's fun while it lasts. And yes, I'm cynical. You meet more frogs than princes in my business. Ever notice how there's an overabundance of amphibians in every fairy tale—and a corresponding drought of royal suitors?

It's a numbers game.

Since it's about a million degrees in Vegas today, we're holding our monthly company meeting lakeside. Despite being as manmade as most Vegas attractions, the lake's gorgeous. After running through our bookings for the next month and brainstorming new party ideas, we've vacated our temporary boardroom (the picnic table underneath a particularly gnarly Joshua tree) for a well-earned swim.

I float in the lake, trying to pretend I'm not still thinking about our financial bottom line and how to drum up more business. Income-wise, we haven't hit survival levels yet. I tilt my head back, and everything's better in my relaxed, upside-down world. My three part-time princesses may moonlight as showgirls on the Strip, but they're paying their bills. Our singing dragon doubles as an Elvis impersonator. He's crooning the King's finest to my accountant. Everybody's taking a moment to let loose just a little and enjoy. We're going to get there eventually—*there* being financial security, fat 401Ks and permanent employment.

In fact, the only person *not* here? Rocker. My business partner and baby brother swore he'd meet us here, but he's once again failed to make an appearance. He's busy at an auto body shop where he does custom paint jobs. Plus, he rides with the Black Dogs MC. He swears the motorcycle club is completely on the up-and-up. According to him, the stuff you see in the TV shows or read about on the internet is 98 percent crap and untrue.

It's the other 2 percent that worries me.

My baby brother now stands a whopping six feet two inches tall. I practically raised Rocker after our parents flaked out on us, and I did the best I could. Money and education—those two things keep you safe, get you out of the lousy neighborhood and into the good places. The princess party business is our first-class ticket out of East Las Vegas to somewhere else. Somewhere safe. I may not know much about clubs or colors, but I do know that bikers are the opposite of safe—and Rocker's been acting secretive.

A splash sounds somewhere south of my feet and someone tugs on my toes. "Cavalry's here."

I sit up fast, butt bumping on the bottom of the lake. Carlie laughs, but she's already staring up the road, longing painted all over her face. My brother turned out to be hot and the bad-boy-biker thing is just the cherry on the sundae as far as some of my employees are concerned. Carlie starts finger-combing her hair and plumping her boobs up in her teeny-tiny bikini top—a definite Rocker alert.

Sure enough, a big, shiny, way-too-loud Harley approaches our temporary campsite at Mach Seven speed. Rocker drives too fast. He also brakes too late and too hard, his tires sending up a cloud of dust as he stops next to the RV. I wade out of the lake, grab my towel and brace myself for the excuses. He's endlessly creative when it comes to explaining his absences.

"Looks like I'm late to the party." A charmingly rueful grin curves Rocker's mouth. Objectively, I see exactly what makes Carlie daydream about my brother.

Dark blond scruff shadows killer high cheekbones and his hair falls around his face in wicked disarray. His legs straddle the bike, encased in worn denim and ending in a pair of impressive black motorcycle boots.

He hops off the bike and sweeps me into a bear hug, grinning down at me. This is why I can't stay mad at him—no matter what we've done or how infrequently we see each other now, he's always glad to see me. He loves me, and he's not afraid to let other people know it. Carlie practically swoons behind me as he plants a gentle kiss on my forehead. A guy who's not afraid to admit his feelings is a prince and is just as rare.

"Fashionably late, Rocker?"

He flicks my nose lightly. "I got held up. Club business."

It's always club business with him. "I needed you here."

He makes a show of looking around the site. "Looks like you've got everything covered."

Uh-huh. We've had this conversation before, and it does not improve with age. "We're supposed to be partners."

"I'm the silent partner who provided the start-up cash. You provided the brains."

He gives me another easy smile, but I can tell he's done discussing this. He's got a point, too. I need a squeaky-clean image to appeal to the mom crowd—so by hanging back, he's actually doing me a favor. Plus, if I push him too hard, he'll just get back on his bike and leave. So I cave.

"You look tired." This isn't a polite lie on my part—

there are purple shadows beneath his eyes and his pretty face is slightly worn.

"Club's keeping me busy." His tone makes it clear that this is another conversational no-fly zone.

"You know you have a job with me anytime you want it." We've had this conversation only about a million times, but it bears repeating. I will always be here for Rocker.

He tilts his head at the RV. "You really see me driving around in that thing?"

"What's wrong with the Princess Mobile?" Admittedly, the gas mileage sucks, but she gets us where we need to go, she's great advertising and she has honest-to-God turrets. Pop that sucker up and I can play Rapunzel on demand. It holds my costumes and props, and it gets my princesses from one party to the next.

Rocker's just starting to list all the reasons a pink ride isn't his thing when his phone goes off. He looks down and then disappears briefly to take the call.

"I have to go," he says, sauntering toward me.

Yeah. Color me shocked.

He pulls me into a one-armed hug. "Be extra careful for me, Evie girl?"

"I'm always careful," I tell him, and sadly, it's the truth. I'm a color-between-the-lines girl—he doesn't need to worry about me.

"Promise me," he insists and I think he's actually serious.

"You want to be more specific?"

He curses. "Evie—"

"Does it have anything to do with your club?" I

point to the patch on his vest. I'd like to rip the thing off his chest, but it wouldn't solve the problem.

"Might do. Trouble's brewing," he says slowly. "Trust me. You don't want the details, Evie. I've got it handled, though. You don't need to worry."

Some things never change—Rocker swears he's got a situation under control, I worry, and then I conceive a half dozen plans for salvaging said situation. I love my baby brother, but I don't approve of his lifestyle choices. His biker buddies are bad news. Today, though, he really doesn't want to talk about whatever's bothering him, so I nod and promise to be extra careful. He gets back on his bike and tears out of the campsite faster than I've ever seen him go. Whatever trouble he's facing down must be really bad.

It's one hell of an exit—even more dramatic than the Princess Mobile. It makes it impossible to ignore his departure, which Samantha makes clear when she wanders over, fanning herself.

"God, your brother's hot."

I force a smile, although the last thing I want to discuss with my fellow princess is the degree of my brother's attractiveness. I've got bigger things to worry about. "In the category of things I don't need to know…"

"Who's hot? And are we sharing secrets?" Carlie wades out of the lake to join us.

"Rocker's in trouble."

Samantha wraps an arm around my shoulders and squeezes gently. "You need to stop worrying about that man. He's an adult, doing adult things."

"Funny. That's *exactly* what I'm worried about. Life was way easier when he was just afraid of the monsters in the closet."

"You should be thinking about dating or at least getting laid," Samantha counters. "Ask Rocker to introduce you to some hot biker."

"No bikers," I say firmly.

"Really?" Carlie sounds doubtful.

Bikers are fascinating, but they're the polar bears of the dating world—a look-don't-touch breed of man you're better off spotting in a zoo than in the wild. So freaking touchable on the outside, but completely wild on the inside. I love bad boys, but I prefer to do my loving from a nice, safe distance.

"*Biker* is a synonym for *bad boy*. I don't need that."

"What if I find you a bad boy with a heart of gold?" Samantha is the eternal optimist.

Reality check. "I'll be ninety before you find one of those. Give me someone who's nice."

"Imagine the sex. Booooring." Samantha makes a face and wades back into the lake. As she executes a spectacular belly flop into the cool water, I check my phone. We need to be on the road in twenty minutes or we'll hit traffic. Still, I can afford five more minutes.

I wade back in and rejoin my girls. "It's been so long since I had sex that I'm not sure I remember how to do it."

Obviously, that's an exaggeration, but both Carlie and Samantha look like I've just announced that there will never, ever be another episode of *Game of Thrones*. Possibly combined with a nationwide shortage of chocolate. And wine. Maybe I could kick a puppy and complete my elevation to total loserdom.

"Who doesn't get laid?" Carlie floats over to me. It feels like high school, except the margaritas are no longer illegal. "Do you have a disease? Or did you take a religious vow when I wasn't around to stop you?"

"Not everyone has to have sex. Not everyone *wants* to." Most days I'm too tired to even think about taking my clothes off, let alone doing so in a sexy fashion and then making sure my man comes. I've been working twelve-hour days for the last eighteen months to get my princess party business off the ground, and my efforts are finally paying off.

"Intervention?" Carlie gives Samantha a look I have no problem interpreting. Neither one of them has a filter and they both have frequent, fantastic sex (at least to hear them tell it—and believe me, they certain don't hesitate to tell).

Samantha nods and heads for her purse. She trots back into the water a few seconds later, phone in her hand, and thumbs like a mad woman. Water-based internet surfing seems like an obvious recipe for disaster—while I wish the good folks at Apple would come up with a waterproof number, so far they've dropped the ball on that particular winner.

"We're finding you a booty call," Samantha announces.

"How about this one?" Carlie taps a picture on the phone, but Samantha's already shaking her head vigorously enough to spray me (and the phone—she really is living dangerously) with water.

"He's a taxi and not a long-haul trucker, if you take my meaning. Eve needs someone with stamina. She has a drought to work off."

I mentally run time trials on my previous two boyfriends for the next few minutes (they'd both qualify for gold in any track-and-field sprinting contest) while Carlie and Samantha review and reject various single men. Eventually they linger on a dark-haired hottie with a nice face and a strong jaw. He's wearing a suit and a tie, although there's always the possibility that's an aberration. Maybe Samantha snapped him at a funeral or a wedding.

"Jack Turner." Samantha taps the screen and Jack zooms into focus. "He runs numbers for a casino. He's twenty-eight, currently single, never married and he has his own place. Rumor has it that he's really, really good at putting his partner first. I like a man with manners."

Nice to know the man has been sexually pre-approved. I examine his face. He looks normal. Of course, Samantha and I have also been up since six, preparing for and then throwing a purple-themed princess celebration for the four-year-old daughter of a blackjack dealer who'd received the tip of a lifetime two weeks ago and decided to invest part of it in his daughter's dream party. It's possible I'm not thinking straight.

"Is he nice?"

Carlie pokes me in the stomach. "Trust me. You want fun, not nice."

Says she. "Why can't he be both? You guys said you could find me a bad boy with a heart of gold."

"We lied for a good cause. It would be like winning the lottery. Don't raise the bar impossibly high for Jack."

"I know nice guys," Samantha announces. Since she's been married and divorced twice and she's not even thirty, I'm skeptical. Her first impressions don't seem to be borne out in the long run.

Carlie reaches for the phone. "Name one who can still make your panties wet just by walking into the room. Evie needs chemistry. Not a nap."

See? She agrees with me. Nice guys are more endangered than the rhino these days.

Samantha looks blank. The way she stares down into the water, you'd think she's expecting a name to float to the top.

Shit. Surely one of us knows a guy who's both dating material *and* nice. Or…maybe not. Maybe finding Mr. Nice is like going to the zoo and hoping to spot a unicorn. Fuck the polar bears—we want mythical creatures.

Samantha waves her phone at me. "I'm texting Jack right now. We can go out next weekend."

If today is Saturday, that gives me at least six nights to find my libido. It has to be here somewhere.

Samantha doesn't look up from her phone. "And don't tell me that you're not free. Our clientele are three to eight years of age. They do not host birthday parties after 10:00 p.m. Ergo, you're free and clear for drinks.

There's no excuse to not go out and have fun. Let loose and forget about your responsibilities for a few hours."

*Fun.*

A simple, three-letter word.

I'd like to pretend I can't remember the last time I had fun because I work so hard and am such an astute businesswoman.

It wouldn't be true. I know *exactly* when I last cut loose, went out and had a few, did some dancing and kissed a boy. I was seventeen and in high school.

Unfortunately, I was also supposed to be at home, watching Rocker while our dad was out taking care of some "business" for his MC. Sucks to be a teenager stuck with babysitting duty when everyone else is out partying. My sneak exit through the window had been awesome up until the moment I returned and discovered our house surrounded by the blue-and-whites. Dear old dad got busted running arms, and I got busted as a deadbeat who'd put having a good time ahead of looking out for her little brother.

That was on me.

And yeah, I know that the ten years that have passed since that night should count for something. That Rocker doesn't blame me for the six months of foster homes he'd survived before I'd turned eighteen and convinced the judge to let him live with me. Six months in which I'd turned my life around, found a job and done everything right.

Rocker and I don't talk about our dad or that night everything changed. Once a month, we send a check to the state prison where dear old dad is serving a twenty-five-to-fifty-year sentence, and he sends back a postcard with a scrawled *thanks*. He also sends the occasional Christmas and birthday card. Mostly, Rocker and I pretend our childhood is a big happy blank. Nothing to write home or talk about—just something we got through on our way to being reasonably happy, productive adults.

At least, that's what I do. I'm a business owner and halfway to a degree in finance at the University of Nevada, Las Vegas. I have a mortgage, a minuscule retirement account and enough shit that I had to rent a medium-sized U-Haul when I moved into my new house. It's wonderful and scary at the same time—I'm so close to finally getting us out of the series of bad neighborhoods and loser streets we've lived on all our life and I should be celebrating. I *should* be able to go out on a Friday night and cut loose for the space of a song or two. And yet I'm so tired that I just want to crawl into bed and sleep instead.

"Jack says he'd love to meet you," Samantha announces triumphantly.

"Okay," I tell her. "I'll do it."

While Samantha texts an opus to Jack and Carlie cackles gleefully next to her, I pack us up. I need to double-check the site, too, and make sure no one's leaving anything behind. I'm busy tying up our loose ends when I hear the small plop from the lake followed by Carlie's giggle and Samantha's curse. Yeah. Guess we'll be stopping by the Apple store, too.

# CHAPTER TWO

*Rev*

I'M NO SUPERHERO. Definitely no Prince Charming. Your first clue is my ride. I'm all about the Harley Davidson—not a fucking white horse in sight. The Hard Riders club president must have ignored that memo when he put me in charge of today's mission, because the woman in front of 837 Second Street is dressed exactly like a princess, right down to the tiara. Although the diamonds have to be fake, like so many things in Vegas, the crown still sparkles in the setting sun. A disorganized mob of small girls in rainbow-colored dresses surrounds her, talking and shrieking in an ungodly racket. Fucking looks like a rainbow exploded everywhere and rained glitter.

"Goddamn," Vik announces loud enough to be heard over the pipe's roar as he pulls his bike into the curb. I kill my engine and follow, both of us focused on the commotion happening on the lawn of the run-down rental. The lawn isn't much to look at—the Nevada sun has cooked the grass to a crispy brown and the place hasn't had a paint job in decades. Two bedrooms, one bath, based on the visible square footage, but gone to seed like a hooker working the nearby Strip, still open for business even though she won't command top dollar. The neighborhood hosts mostly working class, the usual mix of single moms and family units where cheap rentals are always in demand. The place squats on the edge of Hard Rider MC territory, and it might be time to expand our holdings. Claim this block, make it ours, put it back to rights.

I fucking love that idea.

Princess sticks out. The neighbors hanging over the chain link watching the show have dressed down for the heat because East Las Vegas in August is hotter than any armpit of hell I've visited as a US Navy SEAL. Today's audience wears mainly shorts and tank tops. Princess, on the other hand, sports a puffy yellow dress made out of some kind of fluffy shit. The fabric bells out revealing a really nice pair of legs as she gets into it with…a dragon? The thing's about ten feet tall, bright purple, and has a tail with floppy cloth spikes on it. Princess retrieves a ginormous plastic sword from somewhere and proceeds to attack. While I applaud the enthusiasm that makes her tits bounce, she doesn't know the first thing about fighting.

Vik groans. Brother's a fucking drama queen. "I could have taken that dragon in the first twenty seconds."

As the dragon collapses in mock death on the crap lawn, Princess whirls, declaiming something that wins applause from her host of mini-me's. I can't see her face, which is a pity, because her back's damn spectacular. Soft, honey-colored curls are piled up on top of her head, kinda pinned in place by the tiara, and the dress dips all the way to her ass, the straight line of her spine a lick-me-here-big-boy invitation I'd like to take her up on. As I watch, some of those curls go AWOL, bouncing around her face and down her neck. I want to take her apart, undoing first her hair and then her dress. Wouldn't stop either until I had her screaming my name as she came undone in my arms.

"Showgirl?" Vik's mutter interrupts the unwelcome fantasy. Daydreaming on the job is a rookie mistake. We've seen some crazy shit in our day, but this is unfamiliar territory. Since Princess doesn't show so much as an inch of tit and the dress drags on the dead grass rather than stopping two inches short of her ass, I'm certain she isn't working a Vegas show on the Strip. Her audience is our second clue. Third clue? The enormous pink-and-purple inflatable castle poking up over the roof of the house from the backyard and the equally outsized sheet cake with a number 5 candle poking out of the center. We've crashed a birthday party.

"You sure we got the right address?" GPS isn't a magic bullet and maybe we aren't parked in front of Eve Kent's workplace.

Vik leans back on his bike, folding his arms across his chest as he surveys the front lawn. A happy grin lights up his face, because he's definitely enjoying the show and most of the audience is female because hello…birthday party for kids. Vik likes women. Women like him. It all works out, usually with Vik naked, in bed, and banging his newest acquaintance. He may be the vice president of the Hard Rider motorcycle club, but you can bet every one of us gives him shit about the mileage on his dick. "Let's go introduce ourselves."

Vik also subscribes to the *act first, think later* school of thought. Probably explains why our prez put me in charge of this particular mission. If it involves pussy, Vik's gonna want to make a detour before he gets down to business. While he checks out the women on the lawn, I check my phone and confirm we're hitting the right party.

"We can't just go in there and make demands." I do a quick headcount and arrive at fifteen possible adult witnesses in addition to the dragon and the screaming, frosting-smeared horde. Never mind that we're not doing anything illegal—yet.

We're assholes, but we're not criminals. Being a biker isn't a crime, even if the boys in blue sometimes act as if it is. There's no free pass—you earn your place in the Hard Riders MC. To ride with the Hard Riders, you have to be ex-military. Most of us are SEALs or Spec Ops, but we got a few exceptions. We ride in East Las Vegas, but the Vegas area is home to multiple MCs and tensions run high. The steady flow of drugs controlled by Los Angeles–based gangs like the Hells Angels, Mongols, Crips and the Vagos add to the tension. Too many fighters, too little turf. That's a bad fucking recipe right there, and the Black Dogs MC recently made it their personal mission to be a pain in our ass.

Sin City is the country's playground, but almost two

million people also live and work here, just trying to make a decent life for their kids and that's a goddamned right, to my mind. Forty thousand decent, hardworking people in East Las Vegas and almost seven square miles of streets of working-class apartment complexes, bars, liquor stores, check-cashing businesses and single-story adobe ranches with palm trees in the front yards and fucking geraniums in pots. You don't get much more American than that.

We get plenty of people from Nellis Air Force Base, too, people who have either come to serve or to support a loved one who was serving. The Hard Riders MC is behind that shit. Makes our neighbors honorary brothers and so we watch their backs since we've served, too. We're more sinner than saint, but our territory is as free as we can make it from the drugs and violence that plague the rest of Las Vegas.

You prospect and then you patch in and get your colors. Get club ink, too. Our club president likes to call that our bar code—Vik jokes it's our expiration date. You remain in the club until the day you die, and if you screw up, the club cleans up the mess. Locals respect our vests and the club patch. When they see that MC cut, they know we mean business, and they usually get the hell out of our way. You don't disrespect us.

Unless you're Rocker Kent, Eve Kent's baby brother, who rides with the Black Dogs and who's recently decided he and his crew should run illegal street guns through Hard Riders territory. He's the reason we are here. Idiot compounded that brilliant plan by networking with the Colombian drug cartels (he's had a busy

fucking month), and that's trouble the Hard Riders
plan to shut down if we can run him to ground long
enough to talk. We're mature like that—gonna start
with words and then work up to fists. Practically deserve the key to the city for that restraint, but we may
have to make do with Eve. Word on the street is that
her brother checks up on her regularly.

She'd make one hell of a hostage.

"You really think she knows where Rocker's at?"

Vik swings off his bike and leans against it. "Give
it a minute and we'll ask. The show's winding down."

While the knee-high crowd stampedes into the
house after the lady carrying the cake, I keep my eyes
peeled for Rocker. He's shown up at three of his sister's
last four gigs according to a girl who works for her.
Usually slinks in quietly because apparently Eve has
a no-bikes rule—something about us big, bad biker
types scares her mom crowd. If I can catch him now,
it will solve all sorts of problems. Of course, since the
girl in question provided this information after Vik
banged her silly, she may have been just babbling shit.
All that mileage on his dick? Plenty of it is repeat business from happy customers.

My phone buzzes, distracting me from the rapidly
emptying front yard.

How's the party?

*Fucker.*

"Sachs is checking in."

Vik nods, his eyes are glued to a mom in a pair of

pink sweats, a white tank and flip-flops. She looks curvy and sweeter than the cake her kid is mainlining as they disappear into the house—and Vik has always had a sweet tooth. Momma better watch out, or he'll take a bite out of her.

What's up?

Shrieks sound from the backyard, the purple castle rocketing back and forth like it's about to take off. Princess and the dragon disappear inside. I'm getting impatient when Sachs finally texts back.

Had another drive-by. Heading over to check it out. Save me a cupcake.

Ever since the Black Dogs MC hopped into bed with the Colombians, our streets have been heating up. This is the second drive-by in as many weeks, and it's two too many. This shit ends now, and the best way to accomplish that is through Rocker. I don't care if he tenders his resignation to his drug-dealing buddies, or if they take it out of his ass in trade, but he runs no more drugs or guns in Hard Rider territory. It's gonna take the entire club to bring him down without escalating shit to a full-blown war, though—and Sachs has a hair-trigger temper. He's more likely to Rambo his way inside the other clubhouse and do his discussing with his fists.

I text him back.

Wait for backup.

Sachs's only response is a kissy-face emoticon. Someday, his lack of caution is going to bite him on the ass.

"Time to get serious." I throw a leg over my bike. "Take one for the club."

Vik grunts and motions me forward. I may be joking about the kiddo's party, but we both know I'd lay everything on the line for the club. So would Vik. That's how we roll—the club and our brothers come first.

When I stride up the walk, what's left of the peanut gallery hanging over the fence turns to stare, because six feet of former SEAL in motorcycle boots and a club vest makes an impression. Fuck them. I don't try to hide what I am. I'm the MC's muscle. I make some stuff happen—and I make other stuff go away. Whatever my club prez needs, I do—and right now he needs Rocker's buy-in on getting the hell out of our territory and the drug trade.

Since staking out a birthday party for kiddies isn't getting me any closer to this goal, I need to find another way to get to Rocker. I do another quick survey of the house, but there's still no sign of that asshole, and I don't have his number. But I bet Evie knows how to call her brother—and I bet I can motivate her to share. I'm fucking awesome at motivating.

And today's my lucky day because turns out that I don't even have to go in after her. She pops out of the house alone and heads for the pink monstrosity parked by the curb, juggling a plate of cake in flapping plastic wrap. She looks like Christmas and the fucking Tooth Fairy rolled into one, with a dash of Tinkerbell and porn star. Okay. That last bit may be pure fantasy on my part, because she looks as sweet as Vik's MILF in that fluffy-ass get-up. Unless my luck has changed, she's not hiding a dirty girl underneath all that sparkle. I change course and wait on the other side of the pink RV for her.

# CHAPTER THREE

*Eve*

"GOING SOMEWHERE, SUNSHINE?" The deep voice comes out of nowhere and I whirl. Off balance, I promptly trip on my dress and head for the pavement.

An arm fastens around my waist, rescuing me from my imminent face-plant. The plate of cake is plucked from my hands and set down by my feet. Huh. The arm tightens briefly as we dip and it's a big, hard, tattooed, scary-as-shit arm, although the tattoo actually isn't bad. Bold black ink covers the skin between his sleeve and his wrist... Is that a dragon? The animal looks almost Viking. Or as if the beast is seriously contemplating eating anyone who gets too close. If I need to file a police report, I have plenty to say when they ask about distinguishing marks.

The arm's owner is sun-bronzed, and when I inhale, I breathe in leather, oil and something else. That *something else* spells trouble because the scent is hot and male. What my head can't describe, my body recognizes, my libido perking up and demanding we revert to our former bad girl ways. Immediately. My princess costume works better than a chastity belt thanks to all that material, so it's difficult to fully appreciate the hard male body pressed up against my butt, but I make an effort.

Maybe I'm hallucinating because men like this don't exist.

I pinch his arm hard.

"The fuck?" Those two offended words rumble in my ear. I guess he's real after all. He sets me carefully back on my feet and backs up, giving me twelve inches of space. Maybe a whole eighteen. And I mean the distance between us, not anything else, because...

This man is a whole lot of wow. I brace myself against the side of the RV. *Knees don't fail me now.*

His face is way better than his arm. He's a big guy, tall and broad-shouldered, traits that tick all the best boxes on my sexual wish list. He's also more rough than good-looking, with short, dark hair and a cold, watchful expression that never leaves his face as he takes in the happenings on the lawn. Almost military, except that the local air force base would never let this bad boy in. He wears a leather vest covered with patches, a dark T-shirt and jeans that are white around the seams. Despite the full-sleeve tattoo on both arms, I spot no visible piercings, but trust me—he doesn't need the metal to shout trouble.

He braces an arm on either side of my head. Despite his not actually touching me, it suddenly feels like we're naked and he's got his dick inside me. Under other circumstances, I might not mind. Since keeping up appearances in front of my paying public matters, I reach out and give his chest a discreet shove. We have an entire RV between us and any party guests, but I shouldn't take chances.

He doesn't budge. "I need to reach your brother, princess."

There are so many different ways to define *reach*. Still, however you define it, he's not here for me. I know I shouldn't be disappointed about that, but I am.

"You're a friend of Rocker's?"

His face gives nothing away. "We've got business."

I treat myself to a second glance at his leathers, the faded T-shirt that hugs a muscled chest and the boots. God. The *boots*. You know how some boots are made for dancing? These boots are made for pain, for kicking ass and for getting a point across one steel-toed tip at a time. And just in case there's any question at all about where this man falls on the naughty or nice side of things, he rocks a leather vest with a club patch on it. Whatever Rocker's done this time, he's in deep. Pulling him out is going to be a bitch.

Ergo, despite my pressing need to get him away from Perfectly Princess Parties's current place of business, I stall. Big-time. "I don't even know your name."

"Rev. You tell him Rev is looking for him."

I'm pretty sure my mouth hangs open for a minute, because *Rev* looks amused. What kind of a name is that?

Since that's not the kind of thing you ask a man, I go for the obvious. "Why?"

"Club business," he says tightly.

In other words? Penis business. Also known as *none of my business.* I love my brother, but he has his head up his ass about things like sticking on the right side of the law and boy things versus girl things. When I try to duck under Rev's arm, the man moves effortlessly with me. Shit. Pretty soon, we'll start attracting attention.

"If I let him know you're looking, you'll leave?" Giving Rocker a heads-up that trouble is knocking on his door seems like my best two-for-one solution at the moment, so when Rev nods, I fish inside the bodice of my dress. I also do my best to ignore the slow grin spreading across Rev's face as I retrieve my phone from its hiding place. What is it about men and boobs? He doesn't back off and give me any space either, which makes dialing awkward.

"What's up?" Miracle of miracles, Rocker actually answers his phone on the second ring.

"I have a friend of yours here who wants your number," I say carefully. Pretty sure this is the *trouble* he mentioned back at the lake.

"Sure." There's enough background noise for me to be almost certain Rocker's parked at a bar somewhere.

"He says his name is Rev."

As my brother silently digests that revelation, Rev moves closer still and traces a finger over my ear. He smells good, although I wish I didn't have a secret thing for leather and man. Plus, he has no business touching me. I shake my head as if he's some kind of annoying gnat, but he just drops his fingers to my jaw and then plays with my hair as if I'm his own personal toy. Big fingers carefully untangle a snarl and smooth the strands down. I slap at his fingers with my free hand and he grins.

Rocker promptly proves that his brotherly radar still works fine. "He right there?"

"Couldn't get much closer," I tell him.

"Rev's not a nice guy," he says slowly. "And I don't want him around you."

News flash—I've already determined the *not nice* part for myself. In fact, it's probably twelve inches long and located directly behind the zipper of his jeans. I look him up and down, or as much as I can since the man still has me pinned up against the RV. Somehow, I can't work up any indignation. Later, I'll regret letting him walk all over me in public view, but right now I'm enjoying the feel of his big, muscled body touching mine. It's been way too long since I had someone just hold me.

I focus on breathing in, hold for a count of three, and then out, because maybe then I won't say something I shouldn't. "Good to know, but I think he still wants to talk to you."

"*He* absolutely does, princess." Rev plucks the phone out of my hand. While I'm trying to figure out how I feel about that, he and Rocker go back and forth on a possible get together. Rev doesn't stop staring at me, either, one hand braced by my face and the other wrapped around my phone. The man's a talented multitasker, because his fingers keep grazing my cheek, sending little skitters down my spine.

Why am I standing here letting him take charge? *Because you like it,* my bad voice whispers (or shrieks gleefully in my head). *Damn. It.* I reach for his wrist as he signs off the call. I still can't tell if he and Rocker are friends, if Rocker owes him money (which would be a bad idea), or if there's something else entirely between them (which would be even worse). But there's something. There's definitely something.

"Return my phone."

His face doesn't reveal a flicker of emotion. Bet he could make a killing playing poker on the Strip. "This isn't a democracy. You got a pen hiding in that dress, sunshine?"

His gaze flicks over me. Maybe he's looking for said pen—or maybe he just likes looking...at me. Shit. The hard-eyed steely-stare thing he's got going on is not supposed to be a turn-on. My inner bad girl, however, won't be shut down without a fight. *She* thinks we should jump him. Right here on the sunburned, stabby lawn works for that hussy. I opt for going on the defensive.

"Don't call me sunshine."

He shrugs. "You're the one in the big yellow dress."

"Occupational hazard." I yank a business card out of my cleavage and slap it in his empty palm. The move may not be the classiest, but the look on his face is worth it. Naturally, birthday parties for the two- to five-year-old crowd are not his territory. He's undoubtedly more into murder and mayhem.

"You want a princess to grace your next party? I make it happen. Forty dresses that drip sparkles, fairy wings, tiaras and enough faux glass slippers to shoe an entire beauty pageant—we'll have a real good time. I promise."

He makes a rough sound. Can't tell if he's laughing at me or if I've actually managed to shock the big, bad biker. "Since when do princesses have wings?"

Clearly, he has limited knowledge of five-year-old girls.

"All the best princesses can fly," I inform him. Unlike him, I have extensive knowledge of five-year-old girls, and their preference for fairy princesses have been made abundantly clear to me. Ergo, I've responded to my market demands (and hey, I like wings and sparkles, too).

This time, he definitely snorts. "Why don't you fly your ass on inside that RV and grab a pen?"

I don't have to think about that "request" too hard. The man needs to work on his manners.

I don't budge. "Rocker's not your number-one fan."

He grunts and returns his gaze to my phone. "He wants you safe. You should listen to him."

"You should know something about me," I tell him.

"What's that, Evie?"

"I'm not big on orders."

He actually winks at me. "Bet you'd feel differently in bed."

I really shouldn't hit him, not when there's a birthday party happening in the backyard behind us, but the urge is almost overwhelming. This man has no filter. "Do you have any idea how insulting you are?"

He shrugs and texts something from my phone, before looking me in the eye. God, the man might be filterless, but he does have gorgeous eyes. "Put my number in your contacts."

Um. Okay. And perhaps hell will freeze over despite the record hundred-and-something-degrees Vegas weather. I reach for my phone, but he holds it just out of reach. "If I change my position on order-taking, I'll be sure to give you a call."

"Thought maybe we could get together sometime," he says.

Didn't see that one coming.

"You want to go out on a date with me?"

"It's a free country—you don't have to say yes. Thought you might like a ride on my bike or a drink."

*He wants to give. Me. A ride.* My brain stutters. The bike parked by the curb is a big, death-defying, powerful menace. Black leather saddlebags hang off the side that I'd bet my sheet cake he doesn't use to transport groceries or crap from a Target run. Riding anywhere with a strange man would be crazy.

He has a friend with him, too, another man I've never met before. When I peer over Rev's shoulders a little myopically (the best princesses don't pair glasses with fairy wings and this particular princess has run out of disposable contacts), the guy offers me a slow grin and a little waggle of his fingers. He certainly makes pretty eye candy, but I prefer Mr. Tall, Dark and Grumpy.

I narrow my eyes at him. "It's the dress, isn't it?"

He doesn't bother to hide his amusement. "You think I've got a thing for sparkly shit?"

There isn't a man alive who looks rougher and

fiercer than Rev. I'm trying to figure out a polite way
to tell him so when he tucks the phone back inside my
dress before I can so much as squeak out a protest. The
backs of his fingers brush against the top of my boobs,
issuing an invitation of their own.

I have to be more cautious. From the rising volume
of the squeals emanating from the backyard, cake con-
sumption has concluded and the party will be wrapping
up as the sugar highs hit, the early departers fleeing
past my RV parked out front. Spotting the princess in
an R-rated embrace with a biker would be bad for my
business. You can't be a dirty girl and host children's
birthday parties for a living. The moms will kill you.
Fortunately, the moms aren't mind readers. I'm only a
party-perfect princess on the outside. Riding anywhere
with Rev would be career suicide.

My bad voice promptly weighs in. *But only if you
get caught.*

"I don't do bikers."

Something flashes across Rev's face. "You don't
get hurt on my watch. I promise."

"You're not an ax murderer?"

He reaches into his pocket and pulls out the wallet attached to his belt by a silver chain. Silently, he
flips it open and holds it out so I can read his driver's
license. There's a military ID underneath it, too, the
kind of card that gets you into Nellis Air Force Base.

"Your name isn't Rev." According to the State of
Nevada's laminated plastic, he's one Jaxon Brady.

"Road name," he says tersely.

I examine the license again. He's also turning

thirty-three in four weeks. I bet he won't be booking a celebratory princess party.

"Wow." I hand back his wallet. "Former navy?"

He nods, as if it's no big deal. "SEAL. You'd be safe with me."

He's not big on talking. Or negotiating, asking, or sweet-talking. I've always trusted my instincts, though, and right now they're on board with Rev Brady. Completely, totally, 100 percent in favor of getting on this man's bike and riding off with him. Somewhere. Wherever he wants to go. He's big and strong and tempting. He's fought for our country and kept everyone safe.

How bad can he be?

The little voice in my head pipes right up. *How bad do you want him to be?*

That voice needs a gag.

"Think about it," he says and then he turns and saunters toward his bike. I stand there, watching his ass the whole way, and wondering why I don't mind his attitude. He's scary as shit. He's not Mr. White Picket Fence and he's not promising happily ever after, but the man has a fantastic butt and I'm lonely. That's all it is. I need to get out more, need to make a point of seeing someone.

Someone else.

*Anyone* else.

There are absolutely, positively no bikers anywhere in my future.

# CHAPTER FOUR

*Eve*

THE CARNIVAL MUSIC vibrates through every inch of my body, and I lose myself in the beat. I love everything about hitting the Strip, from getting dolled up to the pulse-pounding, searing rhythm of the clubs. Everybody's equal on the dance floor, all part of the same moving, gyrating body. On the Strip, you end up packed too close to even tell who can dance and who's merely enthusiastic. It's exactly what I need, my happy place where I can let go and all that matters is finding my next breath and the rhythm.

Unlike my day-job wear, my dress tonight barely skims my butt. Sequins cover the short pink tank dress and whenever the lights hit me, I light the place up. Over the top? Check. Girly as hell? Check, check. The first stop on tonight's girls' night out is Circus Circus and Samantha and I have already hit the Midway and gone two rounds on the roller coaster. I'm barefoot because I kicked off my shoes as soon as we scored a table, and right now it's officially fun time. And while I usually keep busy, busy, busy, it feels good to have some time off. Tonight I can let go and enjoy life. Tomorrow is soon enough to worry about the bills, the taxes and the fourteen hundred other items on my to-do list.

I could start with that man headed toward our table. He's good-looking, he's definitely friendly and he's managed to hunt down a cocktail waitress with a tray of drinks.

Jack. His name is Jack. I'm too old or too tired—too *something*—because I have to fight the urge to write his name on my hand lest I forget it. I'd been hoping he'd rate higher on the droolworthy factor.

"I told you he was even cuter in person," Samantha crows as she catches me watching Jack. Unlike so many dating app pictures, he actually looks like the picture I picked out on my phone at the lake. Turns out, the six intervening days have not been enough time to rediscover my libido. I've done some solo workouts in bed, but a few self-induced orgasms haven't made me hungrier for one-on-one action. Guess it was like hoping running a mile would prepare me for the marathon—so I shouldn't feel so disappointed.

Jack is a good-looking guy and he has lovely manners as promised. He looks really nice in his jeans and a blue button-up shirt, too. He's a vice president of something at one of the casinos, which means that not only is he pretty on the outside, but he's gainfully employed and scores frequent free drinks. The man is total keeper material, which is exactly what I told Samantha I wanted.

This is torture.

I don't care if Jack never finds our table again, and that's just not right. He's so perfect on paper, and yet there's not a single spark of chemistry between us. There's nothing horribly, wonderfully electric, no sparks. I should try harder. Hell, the *sparks* between that biker and me were enough to start a forest fire or some other kind of world-ending conflagration and my libido needs a good talking-to. *No bikers*.

"Wasn't sure what you'd like," Mr. I'm Perfect On Paper says, tipping the waitress generously after she sets the drinks down on the table. "So I got a bunch of stuff. You can try it all or go for the fallback beer."

God. Could he be more thoughtful?

He gestures toward the row of drinks and I grab the first drink I touch. The crap in the glass is frozen and sweet, some kind of adult slushie. *Okay.* That's a departure from my usual beer, but I definitely want to try new things. I want to dance, to grind against Jack and to discover he's my Mr. Right. I'm so ready to get right on that happily ever after. Get married, start a family, do things right. Jack ticks all the boxes. He's absolutely perfect. I knock back the first inch of my drink, trying to ignore the way it suddenly tastes too sweet.

Jack slides an arm around my shoulders, tucking me against his side. He goes for the beer, and we stand there all couple-like for a long moment, watching Samantha bob and weave across the casino floor to greet someone she knows. It feels as if we've been married for ten years already and not in a good way.

*Run away,* my bad voice whispers.

Not listening.

"Let's dance." I slip out of his hold. The bar and burger joint has live music tonight, and a group of people are already dancing. I grab his hand, threading my fingers through his. He lets me tug him out into the heart of the dance floor, following my lead effortlessly. Maybe it's a sign that I've found a man who can take direction? Jack even turns out to be a decent dancer. We dance a few faster songs, and then sway slowly in place when the band drops a romantic number on us. This is perfect. Still, when the band segues into a faster song, I pop out of his hold.

"Little girls' room," I tell him and he nods.

I make a pit stop at our table for my shoes, which turns out to be the best decision I've made all night. The bathrooms are at the end of a narrow, dirty, dark hallway. Every time I pick my feet up, a sticky, crunching sound assaults my ears and I make a mental note to Lysol the bottom of my shoes when I get home. I do my business as quickly as I can, wash my hands and exit. Clearly, the casino wants its ladies out on the main floor or knocking back drinks at the bar, because absolutely nothing about the grimy, dark facilities encourages you to linger. This place has a pee-and-get-the-hell-out vibe.

When I come out, turns out the night has at least one surprise in store for me. Rev is leaning against the wall opposite the door, beer bottle held loosely in his hand. He raises the bottle in a silent salute when he sees me. *He* doesn't look surprised to see me, although I hadn't pegged him for the club scene. When he takes a swallow from the longneck, the muscles in his throat working, I start wondering what he'd taste like.

"Hey," he says, and my feet immediately cease their forward momentum. I have no idea how he does that to me.

"Hey yourself." I gesture toward him. "You waiting for someone or do you regularly stake out the women's room?"

We've only met once before, but somehow I already know he's not the kind of guy who holds his girl's purse while she pees. Plus, I was the only gal in the restroom, so I've kind of already answered my question.

A slow smile touches his face. "Saw you out there on the dance floor. Bought you a beer." He starts to hand me the second beer bottle and then pauses. "You like that lime crap?"

I make a face before I can stop myself. "Not really."

"Good call." He flicks the offending lime toward a nearby trash can and then swipes his thumb over the mouth of the bottle before passing it to me. "Gotcha covered."

Free beer is always good, right? We drink in strangely companionable silence for a moment.

"You come here often?" I joke lamely when the whole not-speaking thing starts to feel uncomfortable.

He bumps my shoulder companionably with his, gesturing toward the dance floor with his bottle. "Worse places to hang out."

"True," I agree. "But I hadn't pegged you for a clubber."

He takes another swallow of his beer. "I like watching."

He'd said he'd spotted me on the dance floor earlier—did he watch me? Did he like what he saw? Is that what this beer is about, or is he still trying to track down Rocker and he figures buttering me up is a shortcut? Since there's no way to know for certain, I decide to just enjoy the scenery for now because looking at Rev is pretty darn awesome. I let my gaze trail the length of his body, taking him all in—and there's lots to admire. His faded jeans hug powerful thighs and the T-shirt beneath his leather vest outlines a chest that promises to be downright perfect. Whatever the man does with his free time, he doesn't sit around on his ass all day. His big body radiates power, deadly but relaxed enough for now that I don't sprint for the dance floor or the safety in numbers it offers—which makes me as stupid as the slowest gazelle in the pack, because Rev is a predator and we both know it.

About three inches from the bottom of my beer, the band starts in on one of my favorite songs, making my feet itch to be out there on the dance floor. A lazy smile tugs at the corner of Rev's mouth. Whatever he is tonight, he's in no rush and somehow I'm in no hurry to return to Jack, either. When my buzz dies down, this will probably worry me.

His shoulder bumps mine gently. "You in a dancing mood tonight, princess?"

"You dance?" Shoot. I sound breathless.

He takes another swig from his bottle. "Do I look like I dance?"

"Uh—no?" I inspect him again, looking for any reason to say yes. "But you've got two feet, right? It's not hard."

He looks down at me, reaching out to circle my wrist with his fingers. Heat shoots through me. Jack and Samantha probably think I've fallen in or gotten lost, and yet I don't want to move away from Rev. Of course, he's hot and I'm buzzing, but even so I know that standing here with him is a bad idea.

"Come on." He tugs me out of the hallway, then heads for one of the booths lining the side of the bar. Stupidly, I follow along. I do manage to fish in my purse and find my phone so that I can shoot off a quick text to Samantha.

Met friend. BRB.

*Friend* is a misnomer, but since Samantha didn't spot Rev at the birthday party, she wouldn't know who he is anyhow.

Rev slides my purse down my arm and tosses it toward the back of the booth. The little pink square at the end of a silver chain doesn't hold much. I slide in after it and then wonder if I've made a mistake. Now the only way out is through Rev. Not that I really think he'd hurt me, but I barely know him.

"You look nice," he says, snagging my phone and sliding in after me. Somehow, I'm not surprised when he looks down and reads the message I just sent.

"Thanks. Maybe we should talk about boundaries."

He looks up and winks at me. "If you've got hard limits, you tell me."

Did that sound sexual to anyone else?

"We what you said?" He gestures toward the phone in his hand and then tucks it into my purse.

"Friends?"

"Yeah," he says. My beer is mysteriously empty, so I snag his and help myself to a drink. "Never had a girl friend before."

"I'll go easy on you," I tell him and finish off his beer.

His fingers graze the bare skin above my knee. "You here with someone?"

My pulse rockets into overdrive.

"Kind of." I blurt the words out. Think them over. "Not really. Yes. No."

He gives me a slow smile. "Hard to be all of those things."

"I'm here with friends," I say firmly.

He nods thoughtfully. "You should know that if you stay here, I'm gonna want a taste of you."

I stiffen before I can stop myself. This is not the kind of thing you discuss with an almost total stranger. "You did not just say that."

His fingers move a little higher. I slap them and only end up smacking myself. Real smooth. "That's disgusting."

His grin gets broader. "You not a fan of oral, Evie?"

Great. Now my face *and* my pussy are on fire.

"Not really my thing." I blurt the words out before I can think them through.

"Why not?" He sounds thoughtful, rather than pissed off or offended, so I tell him the truth.

"I've tried it, but it wasn't all that." I give my previous boyfriends full points for enthusiasm, but oral sex just isn't the fireworks-inducing pleasure that my *Cosmo* assures me it is. I can and have lived without it for years. There's just something about the enthusiastic licking and the slurping that put me off. Reminds me of puppy dogs or something, and that's not sexy at all.

Rev gives me a look. He's totally still, but somehow I get the feeling he's about to pounce. "We really friends?"

"I think so." I nod cautiously. Probably shouldn't have finished his beer because now the room whirls gently around me and a pillow sounds like nirvana. Bet Rev would let me put my head on his chest. Bet he'd let me do a lot of things.

"Then I gotta tell you something, as a friend." He pulls me onto his lap, settling my back against his chest as he rests his chin on my shoulder. "Fucking waste, your not liking oral."

He doesn't sound mad that I've shot down his *friendly* offer, but this is undoubtedly my cue to go back to my own table. Still, when he pulls me tighter, the closeness doesn't feel scary or like a threat. More like he's putting himself between me and the rest of the world, just in case shit starts happening. Which it probably does in his world, now that I come to think of it.

"So show me how you like it," he rumbles in my ear.

"What?" Pretty sure I sound as dazed as I feel.

He tugs the empty beer bottle away from me and sets it on the table.

"Kiss me the way you'd like to have your pussy kissed," he offers. "Promise you one thing, Evie—I'm a fast learner."

"But I don't like it," I point out with the careful logic of the slightly inebriated. "And we're just friends. Friends don't go down on friends."

Or have conversations about oral techniques in the middle of a bar—but, details.

He sounds sincere when he says, "Nothing wrong with one friend making another feel good."

I think about that while he runs his hands down my back, cupping my butt and lifting me until I'm sitting on his dick. The only things between us are my panties and his jeans. Or wait—maybe he's pro-underwear and not naked underneath his denim? The beer must be talking, because I skim my fingers under the edge of his jeans on an exploratory mission. Not commando. Okay. That's one question settled.

"This is a bad idea," I inform him even as I turn and straddle him. I can't be that drunk, because I manage it without sticking my knees in any unfortunate places. Or maybe that's because his hands guide me and it's so easy to let him take control.

"Never a bad idea to tell me what you want." The words sound like a promise. I lose the thought as I slide my hands up his chest and over his shoulders to cup his neck. God, his skin's warm. I wonder how he feels about licking, because right now his dick is aligned with my pussy and it feels absolutely perfect.

"Plus, sweetheart? I've got one rule. The game stops the minute you tell me you're not having fun."

That's a good rule and I tell him so.

He nudges my chin up until I meet his eyes. "You've got my promise on that."

"And you always keep your promises."

"Damn straight."

He's smiling when he says it, but the words are like a safety line. Nothing too bad can happen now. He's said so.

"First thing? I don't like to rush," I whisper, leaning up.

"Got all the time in the world," he tells me.

No.

He's so wrong.

All I have is right now, this one stolen moment.

I cup his head with my hands, one thumb tracing the soft line of his ear. Must be the only place the man isn't hard, because I'm definitely sitting on an impressive erection and his chest isn't any softer. I tug his head down toward my mouth before I can think too much. He helps me by cupping my butt and boosting me up his chest, his fingers skimming the curve of my butt just below my panties.

"I don't like to go for gold right away." I brush my mouth over his throat. He's inked in so many places. In addition to the dark bands on his wrists and forearms, he's got more ink on his throat.

"This is pretty." I trace the black swirl nearest his ear with my tongue.

"Got nothing on you," he growls. "Girls are pretty."

"Mmmm." I eat him, kissing my way toward his ear. I lick him and he groans.

"Pretend you're a girl," I whisper. "And let me call you pretty."

"Fuck," he says hoarsely. "Asking the impossible, princess. I've definitely got a dick."

The tip of that dick bumps against my clit in a bull's-eye. Nothing subtle about the move, but somehow the very bluntness of it makes me hotter. Plus, he grabs my hips when I buck, holding me rock-steady in his hands. My internal temperature rockets up to *on fire* and it's all I can do to not grind down on him and come right now.

"Are we still playing show-and-tell?" he asks with a hoarse groan. "Because you're giving me ideas."

"Shut up." I lick his ear lightly, teasing him. "This is my show."

"For now," he agrees, making it clear I'm only in control because he's letting me be. That apparently turns me on, too, because my pussy clenches, reaching for the dick I've decided it can't have. Still, since he asked for a lesson in how to lick my pussy, I need to be thorough, right? Just in case we ever end up putting this plan into action, I'd hate to be the one to give him bad advice. So I go back to work on his ear, sucking hard on the lobe until he's the one bucking up. Imagine that. What works for the princess works for the big, bad biker.

"I think we're gonna be real close friends." His hands trace the top of my thong through my dress, and when he tugs gently on the tiny strip, I feel it right in my clit. My panties are his own personal leash to my libido. God, I should get up. Should go. Should—

"You like it slow," he whispers roughly, and my thoughts grind to a happy halt. Right now, I'd like it however he wanted to give it to me.

"My fantasy," I whisper back. "My rules."

"You want to hear about mine?" He wraps my hair around his hand, pulling my head back until I meet his gaze.

"I have friends waiting for me." I sound the opposite of decisive.

"Had a real shitty day, princess," he growls. "Don't make it worse by leaving now."

"Funny," I gasp. "Because mine is getting better by the second."

"Tease," he whispers softly, but he doesn't sound mad any longer. "Didn't think you'd play these kinds of games."

I press down on him. "What kind?"

"The dirty kind."

His fingers tighten in my hair and my heartbeat jacks up, announcing the imminent arrival of my first heart attack. We're in public. Sure, the booth gives us some privacy, but it's nowhere near enough for him to be all but fingering my pussy. Why don't I mind? Why am I still sitting here on his lap, my legs hugging his hips like he's my life raft in the Sea of Orgasm? His legs shift beneath me, the muscles bunching and pressing, and a new heartbeat explodes between my legs. Rev is dirty. Wicked. Biker. Outlaw. All the words drain right out of my head when his hand disappears between us. Oh my God, he's going to touch me.

"Didn't think you'd let me do this."

His fingers stroke beneath the edge of my panties.

"Why not?"

"You usually date bikers?" His fingers move higher. My breath catches.

"I don't usually date," I admit. "Tonight's the first time in a long time for me, and I'm kind of sucking at it."

I should care. I should feel bad that I've left people waiting for me at our table while I climb all over Rev like he's the only orgasm left in town. Instead, all I can feel is the pleasure. He strokes along the crotch of my panties and my world stills and then explodes in a new beat. He works his finger beneath the edge and my pussy rolls out the welcome mat. Like he knows all I can do is wait, holding my breath and trying not to beg, he works the damp cotton against me, rubbing and pressing. They're not even *good* panties, date night panties I wouldn't mind flashing the world, but they're my lifeline in the storm that is Rev. Just an everyday Hanes cotton thong that's practical, sturdy and out of this world in Rev's hands.

"You like these?" He tugs the side of my panties.

"They get the job done," I say drily and he laughs.

"Guess that means you won't miss them."

He rips my panties apart with two sharp tugs and I don't have a problem with that, either. Apparently, I'm up for whatever he wants to do tonight.

"Tell me about your day," I gasp, desperate for distraction. I so need to put the brakes on this crazy attraction.

His knuckle finds my bare clit and presses. It's too much, too fast, his fingers sliding over my slick, wet flesh. I feel my orgasm coming, and I want to stretch this moment out. Make it last as long as possible, because the best sex of my life shouldn't be this short.

"Got some unresolved club business." He circles my clit with his thumb and I reward him with a moan. "Some guys trying to run drugs on our turf. Not good for the neighborhood—civvies keep getting shot."

"You're worried about your neighbors?" It's a minor miracle I can get the words out, because he makes another slow pass around my clit.

He gives me a hard look. "You don't think I should love my neighbor as myself, sunshine?"

Right now, the only *loving* I'm worried about is what's happening between us. He presses. I moan.

"I don't worry, princess. I fix shit."

From the expression on his face, those drug dealers will be out of business shortly. Rev clearly has a plan and a goal for shutting them down and part of me wants to stand up and applaud him. I mean, I probably don't want to know exactly *how* he intends to eliminate the drug trade from the streets he's claimed, but the idea's solid. Instead of saying anything, however, I slide down, more than meeting him halfway. God. I need him in me, and not just his fingers.

A throat clears behind us. "Eve?"

Oh shit. I turn around at light speed, ignoring the way Rev groans when my knee rams into his thigh.

Jack takes an involuntary step backward, looking uncomfortable.

"Hi," I bleat, sounding like the idiot I am.

"I'm headed out." From the way Jack's looking at
us, he knows exactly what we were doing—and he
won't be calling me. "Play some blackjack and then
head home. You okay?"

"Fine. You go on." My face is probably tomato-red.
Jack is the perfect recipe for a forever man, and he's
just busted me humping another guy. It's not like meeting him here at the casino was my idea (thank you,
Samantha), but I still feel bad. I picked him out of the
phone lineup, and now I officially suck. He won't give
me a second chance—and worse? I don't want one.

What I *want* is to come, to demand Rev finish what
he started. We haven't exchanged much small talk,
and we haven't done any of the get-to-know-you stuff
that you're supposed to do *before* you hook up. But I
know some important things about him already. He's
a member of the Hard Riders MC, which means that
he lives for the club and he plays by a code I can't always agree with. He's loyal. He's protective as fuck.
He'll never bring me roses or stop by Hallmark, but
it's not as if I'm planning on doing that for him, either.
I'm an equal opportunity kind of girl and I might be
up for borrowing his penis, but there's no long-term
in dating a biker.

Which is why I scoot off his lap as Jack turns and
walks away. I'll bet he's thinking he had a near miss.
That if I'd hook up with a different guy when we'd
just met that I'd do worse down the road. Rev's phone

buzzes and naturally he checks it. Those fingers moving over the screen were just—

He makes a rough sound. "Got a meeting or we'd be discussing this further."

This is a first. My dating life hasn't been a flaming success, but the guys I've met have been interested in pussy first, fun second and nothing else third. Sometimes, they've mixed it up and put the fun first, but they've never left a sure thing for a meeting.

That's okay.

"Go." I slide out of the booth. Rev is more than a little out of my league. I like playing games, but I'm not even sure this man knows how to play.

"We're good?" He gives me another one of those intent, scary looks. He's big and not particularly happy-looking, and I'm an idiot for grinding on him.

He sighs, as if he can see right inside my head. "You worry too much."

Worrying is part of the natural order of things. I have a long list of shit to deal with, topped by growing my business, dealing with handsy dads and uncles at my princess parties, whether or not my girls will show up for a gig and where my baby brother has taken himself.

"I *plan*," I tell him. "There's a difference."

Some days it doesn't feel like a big one, but it's who I am.

He follows me out of the booth, setting his hands on my hips and drawing me back against him. His dick makes itself at home in the crack of my butt. The man's built like a small mountain.

"You gotta stop thinking about it all."

And then he bends his head toward mine and brushes his lips over my mouth. He's there so fast, I almost think I dreamed it. Just like that, he's taking up all the space and all of my air. My stupid heart races and all I can think about is what kissing Rev will feel like. His lips brush over mine, once, twice. A third time. He sucks my lower lip in, and then he pulls away.

"'Night, sweetheart," he says and heads for the door.

Goddamned biker.

He's gone before I realize he still has my panties.

# CHAPTER FIVE

*Rev*

I LEAVE NOTHING to chance. This is a recipe for fucking disaster, and I don't bake. I also don't cook, and I definitely don't screw up. Must be the finger bang at the club, because I've decided Evie's safety comes first and I've got my eyes and ears in place since Rocker was a no-show at the meeting *he'd* fucking set up to discuss our mutual problem. He needs to understand the Hard Riders aren't backing down. And me? I need to know no one gets close to Evie. If the Colombians come knocking, I'm ready. I followed Evie to her next birthday party gig and stationed myself outside. Don't think the Colombians are gonna smuggle themselves inside in a gift bag, but eyes on the street are a safer bet. Came in a cage, too, so I wouldn't scare Evie's customers off.

Bet most of her mommies wouldn't mind a biker, though. Bet we'd be their favorite flavor of bad.

Evie's been doing her princess thing for a good hour when Rocker pulls up and parks down the street at a discreet distance. I'm leaning against the garage door, watching the house. The prospect on the south end of the street texted me when Rocker turned into the cul-de-sac. The street's full of cars thanks to the birthday party happening in the backyard, which makes it easier for Rocker to hide his bike.

Rocker and I don't have much of an acquaintance, but I've seen him around and I recognize the colors. Plus, he looks like Evie. Got the same color eyes and hair, although after that the resemblance stops. The sunglasses don't hide the hard-eyed gaze he directs as me, but fuck him. I get that he's not happy about my presence here. I feel like shooting his ass, too, but that's not how this game gets played. He nudges the glasses up and tips his head to me in greeting, taking in the balloons bobbing over the mailbox as the screams coming from the backyard assault us both. It's like being locked in the seventh circle of hell.

The smile that curls up the corner of Rocker's mouth doesn't reach his eyes as he braces a boot against the edge of the sidewalk. "Heard you met my sister the other night at the club."

"She's real nice." I shrug casually. We could be two guys exchanging small talk over a couple of beers. "Might be seeing her."

I'll respect his colors up to a point, but not gonna lie—I enjoy needling him. Plus, taking one for the club and spending time with Evie is a win-win situation for me. She's hot as hell. Gotta hand it to Rocker, though— he keeps his cool and nods as if he isn't imagining ripping me apart with his bare hands. Probably running me over with his bike in that fantasy, too.

"Evie's not big on club life. She's not part of this."

"She is now," I tell him. Wish it wasn't true, but I don't believe in denial. "When you got in bed with the Colombians, she stopped being a bystander. If you can tell me straight up that no one's gonna come gunning for her, I'll consider backing the hell off."

"Shit's complicated," Rocker says slowly. "Not saying I don't understand where you're coming from, but it's not as simple as just saying I'm out of the trade."

I need an angle I can work. "Call it what you want, but you're running shit in our territory and the cartel's got their nose in our business. Step one is for you to back the hell off and stay away from what the Hard Riders claim. Step two? Pick a new career, because drug dealing isn't a long-term proposition. If I don't shoot you first, there's gonna be a long line behind me."

Rocker rolls his shoulders. Must have a knot there the size of a fucking tree, because he does it again.

"Shit's complicated," he repeats. "But I don't want anything happening to Evie. That point's nonnegotiable."

"I'm making her my girl." I usually take my time and think shit over, but claiming Evie feels right. "Not saying she's my old lady just yet, but she's with me. I'll look out for her. You don't come round her until you've got the cartel off your back. You don't talk to her, don't hang with her, don't come near her."

"She's my sister." Rocker crosses his arms over his

chest. Evie's a small woman, but her brother's built like a fucking mountain man. Not that I'm intimidated, but knocking him on his ass will take time and Evie's bound to notice. Plus, I'm pretty sure the princess party people would frown on violence. Could probably start a line of parties for boys, though—maybe I should mention it to Evie. Do some MMA fighting demonstrations. Help her branch out and shit.

"Evie's a big girl—old enough to make her own dating choices."

Rocker studies me. Got no idea what he sees and I wouldn't care except Evie seems to have some inconveniently fond feelings for the fuck, which means I can't just kill him. Pretty sure she's gonna get pissed if I even ding him.

"True," he says finally. "So she talks to who she wants to talk to—you don't get to be the bouncer at the door and run me off. There's no chance she's gonna agree to be your old lady, and you need her okay for any other kind of relationship, you feel me?"

The unspoken *or I'll shoot you* hangs in the air between us. Guess we have something in common after all.

"And you don't get to sell your bullshit on my streets." I'll see his threat with one of my own.

"I'd like to say I don't give a shit about what my sister gets up to with you," he says slowly. "But that wouldn't be true. She's a good woman and she deserves nothing but the best. If that's what you are, I'd be happy to slap a bow on your ass."

I flip him the bird. "I look best in blue."

"You hurt her, and that blue will be a coffin lining, you feel me?"

"Right back at you."

"In fact, keep your hands off her entirely. Keep a couple of feet between you and I won't come back and kill you."

We're still staring at each other, and I'm calculating the chances we go at each other, when the first kids and moms flood out of the house waving plastic bags full of sparkly shit and paper plates of cupcakes. Princess Number One rocks a purple number, while her princess companion sports yellow. The rainbow effect is blinding. The mom stops dead when she spots Rocker and me, sweeping her girls behind her. Bet she's reaching for her phone.

Rocker must come to the same conclusion that I do, because he flicks me a salute and saunters back down the street. Seconds later, he's off on his hog and the princesses are staring after him open-mouthed. Bet Evie kicks his ass for bringing a bike anywhere near her party.

"Does he work with you?" Momma Princess isn't ready to let go of either her suspicions or her cell phone. Ten dollars says she's got 9 and 1 pushed, with that last digit cranked up and ready to go.

"Boy parties," I tell her.

"We could do that for my party," the purple princess stage whispers, tugging on her momma. "Because girls can do whatever boys do."

Momma Princess blinks, but it's not like she can deny logic like that. Kids see the bikes and think *fun ride*—the parents are the ones who jump straight to felonies and jailbait.

"Let me find a card," I say with a straight face.

"I've got a cupcake," the mini-me announces and holds her plate up for my inspection. "You can have it as a down payment."

Kid's gonna be a master negotiator someday. I take the cupcake while it's still on offer and before she starts laying down terms. Chocolate with chocolate frosting—fucking awesome.

"Can you come to my party next week?" Mini-me proves she's smart, going on the attack as soon as my mouth is full of her cupcake. Momma Princess shoots me a nervous look and beats a hasty retreat. Naturally, this is when Evie comes flouncing out of the party looking ready to bust my balls. Bet she heard the bike—which means I'm blaming Rocker. *Fucker*.

# CHAPTER SIX

*Eve*

"Was that *Rocker?*" I clutch my phone so tight that the case bites into my fingers. I'm surprised it doesn't fly out of my hand with the force of my grip—and frankly, I suspect I should be aiming it at the biker lounging against the Princess Mobile.

Rev actually finishes his cupcake before he bothers responding. "He came by," he growls, jerking his thumb up the street.

"And then he just left?" Although Rocker is the silent partner in our party business and his job description is limited to behind-the-scenes stuff like moving heavy objects and paperwork, my baby brother is super protective of me. He's never quite gotten the memo that it's my job to look after him—so he likes to show up occasionally and poke his nose in my business. For him to light out without so much as talking to me is highly unusual and I know exactly who to blame. The mom and the baby princess hovering near Rev must register the tension between the two of us, because they skedaddle for a battered minivan parked curbside.

"No shit." I blame this entirely on Rev. It's not difficult to imagine how his meet-up with my brother went—both of them act like dogs and I'm a hotly contested tree.

"He came by to see me."

I'm trying to give Rev the benefit of the doubt. I'm not under any illusions that he's a good guy, but maybe this isn't as bad as it seems. Perhaps Rocker got a call and will be back in a few minutes. Perhaps he went to pick up something. Okay. I'm stretching and I can admit it.

"You ready to roll?" Rev ignores my last comment.

"That wasn't a question," I grit out. "That was my *brother* who stopped by to see *me*. Why did you run him off?"

We're starting to attract attention. I'm not kidding myself—the dress helps, as does the bright pink RV, but the star attraction here is Rev. More than one of the departing mothers glances sidewise at him as they shepherd their little darlings down the driveway. The man is undeniably hot. Maybe it's the casual power in the way he stands or the stubble that roughens his jaw. There's nothing soft about Rev and absolutely everything about him screams dirty sex. I squeeze my thighs together, grateful for the dress that hides the betraying motion. God, I want this man. We don't have much of a history together and he won't remember my name in a year, but right now none of that matters and that's a problem.

"It's not safe for you to hang around him," he says. At least Rev has the decency to not lie to me about having run Rocker off. Or maybe he knows he's busted and not getting out of this one.

"The lack of detail is not helping your case," I tell him, trying really hard not to stare at his thighs. Or his hands. There's a whole lot of sexy real estate to choose from.

"I'm going to find out what's going on," I continue. "You might as well tell me."

He makes a rough sound that absolutely, totally does not make my panties wet. Much. "Ask Rocker."

"You ran him off—that makes this your problem."

He nods slowly. "You know that your brother rides with the Black Dogs, right? He patched in with them a couple of years ago."

"Unfortunately, yes." I've done some asking around—wouldn't you?—and so far I haven't discovered any magic escape clause. It sure seems like membership in an MC is pretty much a lifetime commitment until death do you part.

"Your brother's been a busy boy. He cut a deal with a Colombian cartel to move their product, but then he tried to cut them *out* of the picture."

I try and fail to imagine my baby brother as a drug dealer. I mean, he doesn't even smoke—how can he be committing felonies on that kind of level? *You know he's up to something.* He was worried out at the lake, sure, but would he really do *this*?

"My brother wouldn't have anything to do with drugs."

Rev looks pained. "Loyalty's good, princess, but you need to keep your eyes open, too. Ask him what's up."

Rev doesn't sound like he's bluffing. In fact, he sounds way too confident. This is *Rocker* we're talking about. I mean, he colors out of the lines a little, but this would be the equivalent of taking a black Sharpie to the whole goddamned coloring book. If I knew for certain he was selling drugs, I'd have to do something. Drugs hurt innocent people. Drugs mean money, violence and turf wars. I've lived in East Las Vegas long enough to know that.

"Come for a ride with me." Rev changes tactics. "I'll drop you at your place afterward. It'll be fun."

"Does the caveman approach usually work for you?"

He shrugs. "It's just a ride."

Uh-huh. "You have a bridge you want to sell me, too?"

As much as I'd like to continue living in the land of denial—the weather's awesome and orgasms for all—I'm a realist. This man wants something. I just don't know if it has something to do with Rocker, my panties, or both. Maybe he wants to pick up where we left off the other night, or maybe there's something else going on here.

"Ride with me," he says, sounding a little impatient. "I promise you'll enjoy the fuck out of it, Evie."

*So sexy.*

*So wrong.*

This has to explain my answer. "Pick me up at six."

# CHAPTER SEVEN

*Eve*

NO ONE WARNED me that straddling a Harley with a hot guy is like using a gigantic vibrator as your pony ride. As a kid, I used to shove a broomstick between my legs and gallop up and down the yard in pursuit of runaway cattle, ponies, and bad guys. Riding with Rev is the grown-up version of that game and different from any other bike ride I've ever taken. As soon as I slide my arms around his waist, locking my fingers just above his belt buckle, he takes off.

*Slow* isn't part of the man's vocabulary. His speedometer never drops below sixty. He takes us out into the desert, the big bike eating up the asphalt with blinding speed. Even through the helmet, the wind whips at my face, tears my hair, chokes my voice in my throat. It's terrifying. It's the best feeling ever. My heart pounds in my ears and an answering pulse springs to life between my legs. My pussy clenches with each turn Rev takes, a hot, heavy beat anticipating the way his body leans into the road's curves, the muscles in his body flexing as he guides us faster, harder, tighter.

When finally we pull over I'm not sure if my throat is hoarse from screaming—or from holding back my moans. Damn, I'm horny.

My partner in crime, however, is oblivious. He waves a big hand toward the open air in front of us. "Lookout."

Since that appears to be a noun and not a verb, I follow his fingers pointing off into space. I don't want to admire canyons or vistas or (frankly) anything other than his dick. I don't even need him to come for me—I just want those big, rough, banged-up fingers shoved inside me and I can do the rest. Apparently, *all* of me wants to live dangerously, not just the part that thought it was a great idea to get on a Harley with this man.

"Thanks." *For nothing.*

I hop off his bike, not sure my legs will hold me. I should be glad he's hands-off. That his definition of *ride* is textbook nice and not a dirty, filthy, orgasm-filled euphemism. Should be. Am not.

I'm such a liar.

I stroll over to the railing and look out. The view is pretty. I even whip out my phone and snap a picture. See? I'm absolutely enjoying my ride. This fun companionship is what I need.

Not sex.

And definitely not sex with Rev.

"Like what you see?" His rough voice rolls out of the silence behind me. It sounds lower, deeper, *darker* than before. I'm not sure he's actually talking about the canyons and the desert at all. Or maybe that's wishful thinking combined with the heat.

Because it's hot out here. I lift a hand to fan myself, tilting my face into the weak draft of cooler air as I tug open the leather jacket Rev insisted I wear. Jeans and boots in Nevada in the summer? I'm definitely overheated.

I don't hear him move. One moment he's still straddling that big, too-hot bike of his and the next he's right up behind me, his thighs pressed against mine, his arms caging me against the railing.

"I like what I see." He growls the words, his mouth trailing over the damp skin of my throat. He does? Heat flashes through my body as I spontaneously combust.

His mouth moves down. "I want you, princess."

My mouth opens and I'm sure there are a dozen witty, sexy, fabulous responses to his statement—but I draw a blank. Suck in air and stare down at his hands wrapped around the railing.

Those hands could be wrapped around me.

Say *yes*.

"It's a bad idea," I say instead. See? I'm being responsible. Mature. Putting my job first. My pussy all but whimpers in protest.

"No one has to know," he counters. The man must be the devil. Or omniscient. A mind reader. It would make for awesome sex but is the risk worth the reward?

"I'll make it good for you," he promises. "I'll be your dirty little secret. Don't you want to come right now?"

Hell *yes* I do.

"Just once?" Because tonight I'm feeling greedy. If you're going off the diet, diving face-first into the three-layer chocolate cake that's been teasing you all day, you don't want just one slice. You want the whole thing. You want to eat until you can't swallow one more bite, until just the smell of all that sweet makes you sick, until you're over it. Done. Kaput.

Rev's my cake.

I've been so good and now, just this once, I'm breaking all my rules and I get to taste him. Lick him. Devour him whole. By tomorrow, I'll be cured of this obsessive need to eat him up, to find out if his skin can possibly taste as good as it looks. Tomorrow, I'll see him and be all ho-hum, been there, done that, couldn't possibly have another bite. We'll be over.

Tonight... I want it all.

All of him.

Once can't possibly be enough, not with Rev.

His slow grin makes my panties wetter. As if I wasn't soaked already from the ride. "How many orgasms you want?"

Maybe I don't need to give him a number. Maybe he isn't cake, but is instead an all-you-can-eat buffet and I can go back for more, more, more whenever I want. That so works for me.

I lean up and nip his bottom lip. "Surprise me."

His eyes darken. "You got any hard limits I should know about?"

I lick where I bit because why play safe now? "Stay the hell away from my ass. Otherwise, I'll give you a play-by-play update."

Some stuff I'm just not into—and something tells me this man has no limits whatsoever. Adventurous is good, but I still have to ride his bike back to my house. Of course, I could take him there, too. Have sex in an actual bed with sheets and pillows and something cushier than the ground but...he's not a keeper man. This is a onetime thing and I don't want him there in my space. I need an orgasm, not memories.

"Gotcha." He gives me a quick, hard kiss, his lips pressing against mine with erotic intensity before they release me. Nope. I don't want him to let go. Not yet.

I reach for his shoulders and he laughs, scooping me up in his arms. He stops to grab his saddlebag— maybe it's the biker equivalent of a toy box because a girl can hope, right?—and then he's effortlessly striding down a small ravine just out of sight of the highway. I probably should worry. Hello, this is bad movie material right here. I've just given him a free pass to have his wicked way with me and bikers aren't particularly known for their upstanding moral values. And yet... I feel free. Free and somehow safe at the same time because whatever Rev does to me, I trust him not to hurt me.

*Rev*

I should kiss her.

Trot out all the tricks I've learned from fucking too many women on too many different nights. Give her the orgasms she's all but begging for and mark her as mine. Somehow, though, the smooth, practiced moves disappear from my head and all I can do is enjoy being here with her, right now, right this moment. I've driven out to the lookout before, although I've never tapped ass here. Doesn't take a genius to know, however, that we need to get off the road for this. Don't know why she's suddenly so impatient, but I roll with it, carrying her down a small ravine. As soon as we're out of sight of the road, I drop my saddlebag and shift her in my arms so I can peel my jacket off to use as a blanket. She's working out of hers, too, so maybe we don't end up with dirt where dirt has no business going.

Her hands start on my shirt next, trying to get the hem up, but that's not how I want this to go. So when she starts snapping out commands to go faster, get naked, do this, do that, I kiss her hard. My mouth covers her mouth, my lips parting hers, as I pour myself into the kiss. She tastes good, like mint and sweet tea. Fuck, maybe she tastes like sunshine or whiskey or any one of a dozen things, but I know one thing for certain. Evie's my Kryptonite. I lay her down without breaking our kiss, planting myself between her legs, cupping her head between my hands as I bury my fingers in her pretty hair. I devour her, pressing my dick against her pussy as her legs wrap around my hips. Fuck, she's greedy.

Love that about her, even though the L-word isn't one I trot out about sex or women.

She swallows a moan when I finally tear my mouth away, leaning back. She's wearing too many clothes and I need her naked. If I start tearing shit, however, we're gonna have a problem with the drive back to

Vegas. I'd enjoy the shit out of her riding naked behind me but we'd definitely attract attention. Plus, I bet that's one of those hard limit things she mentioned. No Lady Godiva on my bike.

"Don't stop," she orders, eyes half-closed. Her hands go to the waist of her jeans, unbuttoning and shoving the denim down. If I don't hurry, she won't wait for me. "You owe me an orgasm."

"Never broke a promise yet," I tell her. She toes her jeans off, but her panties are mine. I tear them off her because they're the cutest little thing—and my souvenir. Perfect spank bank material for later. Gonna wrap that silky blue-and-white scrap around my dick and rub one out—dessert to go, for later. I shove them in my jacket. My next step in this erotic battle we're fighting has to be her tits.

Fun fact of the day—Evie's tits drive me crazy.

I've jerked off to the fantasy of ripping off her shirt, tearing open her bra, and then ramming myself between her breasts, shoving my dick up the tight, sweat-slicked valley until my head hits her lips and she opens up for me. She swallows a moan as I make the first part of my multistep plan reality rather than fiction. I drag her shirt up, and then fuck it, I leave the cotton tangled around her arms, her wrists stretched over her head, braceleted in one hand of mine. Don't need ropes when I've got her like this.

Hot.

Eager.

And all for me.

I unbuckle, unzip and shove my jeans down just enough to get my dick out.

"Hurry," she whispers as if she's got a schedule, a plan, a time table in her head. Fuck doing this on Fast-forward when I could hit Pause and enjoy her for hours. I want her screaming my name, desperate for me, knowing exactly who has his hands, his tongue, his dick all over her sweet, needy body. If she has an itch to scratch, I'm in no position to judge—but I'll make damn certain she knows who's making her fantasies come to life.

I drag the fingers of my free hand down her chest, between her tits, until I'm cupping her, my thumb teasing her nipples. She rewards me with a whimper.

Not good enough.

Her tits are fucking gorgeous, big enough to fill my palms but small enough that I can cup them. Lying on her back pushes her tits up and out, putting those sweet curves on display for me and I'm gonna need both hands to appreciate her right. I give her wrists a gentle squeeze. "Don't move."

Her eyes narrow as her fingers tangle with mine. "Orders?"

Woman's a total back seat driver. We'll work on that.

"Yeah." I lean down and give her another quick, hard kiss. "You got one job here and that's to take what I've got to give you."

She shifts beneath me, stretching, making space for herself. "And what if I don't like it?"

"You've got words. Fucking use them." Not as if

she's held back in the mouthy department before, so she can tell me if something I do fails to get her off. If I don't make this good for her, I deserve everything she can dish out.

Her fingers fall away from mine. "Okay."

"You want me dirty?"

Guess she hears the challenge in my words because her eyes darken and flick down my body. No way she misses the bulge in the front of my jeans.

"Yes. Touch me," she demands. Doesn't move her hands, though, so she definitely deserves a reward.

"Hold your tits for me."

She shakes off her shirt, lowers her hands and squeezes her tits together around my dick. Love how she takes instruction. Since I first saw her, I've been fantasizing about getting her naked. Opening her up, putting myself inside her.

I straddle her, bracing my hands on either side of her head. Spread out on my jacket, strands of her hair tease my fingers, wrapping themselves around me. There's a lesson there. She's the one who's really in charge here.

I wish I could draw this moment out forever, wish I could whip out my phone and snap a picture of her body welcoming mine. Fuck. She feels amazing. I drive forward, her tits hold me tight, and my eyes all but roll back in my head. Gotta get it together. Gotta do her right, make this good for her.

And then she licks the tip of my dick.

I give it to her harder, faster, pistoning my dick in and out of the snug channel she's made for me. Fuck if I can hold back—or want to. I find a rhythm that makes my dick happy, the slick, tight grasp of her skin on mine pushing me higher, tighter, closer.

"This work for you?" I whisper.

She flashes me a grin. "Who wants his happy ending?"

That's all the warning she gives me before she sucks the tip of my dick into her mouth, the head disappearing beneath the perfect O of her lips. Fuck. Me. I'm hard as nails, rough as shit, and she opens wider, swallowing me down. I must look like some monster beast, crouched over her, fucking her mouth, and I don't care. She lets me and I'm far too close to coming.

Fuck happy endings—this is heaven.

I bump against the back of her throat and she doesn't tell me no—just groans and sucks harder like she loves the taste of me. I'm going to blow all over her face, mark her with my come. Her lashes drift down, hiding her eyes from me. Not sure what I expect to see to be honest, but looking at her is sexy as hell.

Fuck this.

I'm not coming until I'm balls-deep inside her, which makes it her turn.

I drop and roll, pulling her over me. Her legs hug my face, her pussy planted above my mouth. She squeals, bracing herself on her arms. Guess she didn't see that coming, but then she whimpers, her thighs trembling, and I cup her sweet little ass with my hands.

"I've got you."

*Let go.*

*Let me.*

She asked for it dirty and I'm just giving her what

she wants. Making sure she's ready before I tap her. And because the taste of her is addictive and I'm not ready to be done. She relaxes in my grip and I part her with my fingers. Another whimper. A sexy-as-hell moan. Her pussy's the prettiest shade of pink, her bush neatly trimmed into a dark arrow of soft hair. Not bare, not quite, just a fucking tease to look at.

"Look at you." I blow lightly, trailing my finger-tips over her folds.

"Rev—" She shudders.

Yeah, she likes this.

Bet she likes this even more. Bet I do, too. I lean in and get my first taste of her. I pull her wide and lick her slowly over and over. When she's squirming, I suck her clit, alternating between the two until she's gasping, her breath catching as I push her closer and closer to the edge. Her tits heave up and down, still wet from my kisses.

I pull away before she comes, grabbing a condom and ripping the package open. Fuck finesse. I need to be inside her *now*. Playing dirty games doesn't mean putting her at risk. I get the condom out, roll it down my dick and yank her down my body. Seconds later I'm pushing my way inside her body.

*Eve*

Rev's monster dick opens me up.

He's big.

It's not like his proportions are a revelation. Deep-throating him wasn't an option, so it's no surprise it takes him long, fabulous, thank-you-Jesus minutes to work himself inside me. He's not holding back, he's giving it to me good, but he's not in any rush, either. He doesn't slam deep, doesn't force my body to yield.

He just waits me out.

I soften around him—he moves deeper. Cause and effect.

My legs open wider, hugging his hips, bumping into the ground, and he grunts, catching my knees with his palms. Putting himself between me and the dirt. I use my new leverage to ride him hard. I don't want slow, I don't want sweet and gentle. Fortunately, he's in the mood to give me exactly what I want.

He slams up and I meet his thrust, coming down hard. A shriek forces itself from my throat, but to hell with it. The sensation is so good. I feel him everywhere, inside, outside, in my head and right goddamned there between my legs. I brace my hands on his shoulders, and yes I dig in with my nails. We're both going to bear marks tomorrow.

"Eyes open," he grunts when my lashes drift down. Not sure what he thinks I'm really looking at because right now all I can do is feel. And feel and feel.

His eyes watch me, dark and intense with need and emotions I can't interpret. He's so different from anyone else I've done this with. He's more in control of this, of *us*, than I like but it's too late to stop, to step back, to hold off the orgasm building deep within me. He so wins this battle we're fighting between us.

"Come," he orders, sliding a hand free to find and press my clit as he drives inside me. God. He fills me up. There's no room left, so I do the only thing I can and come apart. I let everything go and scream with the pleasure, the desire, the feeling of fucking flying and flying, knowing he's here to catch me. It's too much, too everything—too fast and definitely too close.

He grunts something, moving faster and harder, his hands grasping my hips and holding me tight. My head hits his chest, my face pressed against his sweat-slicked skin and I breathe him in as he pounds deeper, finding his own release. I lie there and let him do what he wants with me.

God, he's dangerous.

And then I can't think anymore because his fingers find my clit again and press and just like that I'm soaring, flying and fighting with him toward another release.

*Rev*

Christ. What just happened here?

I wrap my arms around Evie, holding her tight, and try to figure out when dirty sex took a dangerous right-hand turn into something…else. Not sure what to fucking call it, but all I know is that I'm not done with her. She sags against my chest, her face buried against my skin, her hair tickling my nose.

"Rev?" Her voice floats up at me.

"Yeah?" I can feel a smile tugging at the corners of my mouth. I'll tell her whatever she wants to hear. Fucking gospel truth right there. She's amazing. I run my hands over her bare skin. We need to find a bed stat because the shit I want to do to her, with her deserves that much.

"You give good dirty sex," she whispers, rolling off me and standing up. The. Fuck?

I'm not done with her.

Not even close.

But she's already pulling on her jeans, wiggling and tugging, zipping and buttoning. She's not thinking about what else I could do for her. Now I'm just her ride back to Vegas, and maybe, if I did this right, a happy memory. I'm her been there, done that boy. Her past.

She asked for dirty sex, so I'm not sure why *I* suddenly feel dirty. Yes, I'm her not-so-fucking-little secret and that part's okay because it's what I agreed to after all, but I'd also like to do her in a bed, and not some forty-buck-a-night motel, either. Satin sheets, fucking candles—the whole nine yards before I give her the twelve inches that has her name written all over it.

Except she really doesn't want that. Has to be a first in my life, that a woman doesn't want a repeat from me.

"Thanks," she says and heads for my bike. Feels like she slapped me on the ass and sent me on my way.

What the fuck just happened?

# CHAPTER EIGHT

*Rev*

SOME CLUB BROTHERS have permanent women in their lives, old ladies they love and protect. It's a hell of a choice to make and not the kind of shit you can end in divorce court. The day your woman puts on your patch, you take 100 percent responsibility for her actions. She screws up—you pay. That takes more trust than there's gold in Fort Knox. There's nothing easy about being a woman in an MC. We're ornery, protective, and don't just demand respect—we fucking earn it. Play in our world and play by our rules. Not too many women can or will do it.

My future holds no old lady.

No keeper girl.

Evie Kent is a blip on the radar, a pothole in the highway of life. We have no future together. She's untouchable, off-limits, property-of-someone-else material. She made that perfectly clear when she banged my brains out and proceeded on her way as if taking my dick deep inside her meant absolutely nothing at all.

She's right.

Abso-fucking-lutely correct.

What went down on our ride was just sex—and *not* the reason my bike is parked across the street from her house when I could just order a prospect to watch her. Worse, I'm phone in hand, thumb poised to tap her name in my contacts.

Rocker's not on board with ditching the cartel. It will take weeks or months to straighten his shit out. On the other hand, sticking close to Evie will make it easier to discover Rocker's plans. If the Colombian cartel makes a move on her, I'll be in place. And what's the easiest way to stay close?

Make her believe I'm dating material not a quick bang.

We all see the problem here, right?

I don't date.

Ever.

I am, for all intents and purposes, a dating virgin. Dating has the learning curve of nuclear physics—not the kind of shit you casually pick up over the week-end. Sure, fucking Evie Kent would rock, but I hadn't been planning on date nights—or sexting, flirty looks and too-casual questions about the gals hanging at the clubhouse. Phone chats, shared plans and sleepovers? Also not on my to-do list.

Yet here I am.

Waiting on the curb.

Her place looks real cute. No kids, no cats or dogs, but bright red flowers march up the walkway next to a stupid-ass have-a-nice-day flag. She grows roses and owns wicker furniture with matching goddamned pillows. My throat actually itches and starts to close up at all this happy Suzy Homemaker shit.

Before I can text, she pops out, hauling a trash bag half her size. Her tiny cotton shorts don't quite cover an ass that's even sexier than I remember. The shorts are either way too small or they shrank in the wash. Or fuck me, maybe she chose them on purpose to drive me crazy.

Her evil plan is definitely working.

She flips open the trash can, going on tiptoe. The shorts get shorter—my view gets hotter. And yeah, I debate taking a picture since I have my phone handy. Decide against going all paparazzi on her ass because stalking isn't wooing. She tosses the bag, slams the lid shut and starts back to the house.

Stops.

I am pretty hard to miss.

Just in case she's short-sighted, I waggle my fingers at her. She flips me the bird and marches into the house while my head replays every ass fantasy I've ever had.

My phone buzzes.

EVIE: You're a stalker now too?

ME: Just in the neighborhood.

I tap the smiley face button in my message app. Turns out there's a million little pictures you can add to your message, most of which make absolutely no sense. Who the fuck needs pictures of bananas or broccoli? I pick one and hit Send.

And wait.

Maybe she's writing *War and Peace*. Or maybe she's taking a nap. On her bed in those sexy little shorts. I imagine a half dozen ways to peel those shorts down her legs. As the minutes tick closer to a half hour, however, I run out of patience.

ME: Should I apologize?

I'm not sorry at all for fucking her when she gave me the green light, but if she needs to hear the words, I'll give them to her.

EVIE: You move fast

If that's a complaint, I can happily spend longer eating her pussy. I'm still typing my text message when UPS pulls up and Mr. Brown bounds out carrying an enormous pink box. He rings the bell, drops his load on the doormat and leaves. While my inner caveman rejoices he's gone, the rest of me wants more service. This is my grand gesture, after all. I need delivery with a fucking mariachi band and a big bouquet of overdone from the florist. Fireworks and a rocket launcher. Your standard dating shit.

ME: It's safe

EVIE: Not scared

And because my Evie's a doer and not just a talker, she yanks opens the door and stares down at the box. My dick promptly gets hard imagining what's in the box. Her gaze finds me as the delivery truck pulls away.

Yes, I ordered her stuff. I tore her panties off her. I owe her new ones. Plus, shopping's hard to stop. I got started. Each picture I clicked on the website became my new favorite fantasy. If Victoria's Secret let you drag your girl's face over the model's, they'd sell a shit-ton more underwear.

ME: Open it and send me some pictures?

I make it a request. I may be stuck across the street, but I'm getting a handle on this dating stuff. I cross my legs and lean back against my bike. A few seconds later, my phone buzzes with an incoming text.

She's sent me a picture.

Of her middle finger.

I so like this girl.

Her door reopens and her ass appears first. No matter how fast she stripped, I don't think she's had time to put my stuff on. We'll have to work on that. If we're dating, she needs to appreciate what I do for her.

She's carrying a tray with two glasses of something brown with ice cubes. She sets it down, drops onto one of the chairs, and then looks at me and pats the cushions of the seat next to her. Apparently, my dick *can* get harder. Walking across the street is downright painful.

She crosses her legs when I get close. My gaze follows. *Big mistake*. Her left thigh brushes the top of her right, where I've had my fingers, run my tongue up her silky-smooth skin and hit the jackpot. No way she misses my reaction to that memory, because she's sitting in the chair closest to the door and an escape route—so I have to brush past her to sit down. God bless the total lack of space because my erection rubs against her shoulder.

She sighs. "You're impossible."

Complaint or not—you be the judge. I sit, knees brushing hers as I angle the seat closer to hers. Be happy to pull her into my lap if that was what she wanted.

She hands me a glass of tea and launches her opening salvo. "You can't send me underwear."

"Already did." I knock back half my tea. It's actually not bad. Hanging around on the curb is hot work.

"Return it." She launches into a stream of blah blah blah about not accepting presents from me and it's totally inappropriate and how did I know her size because that's creepy (I've had my hands all over her ass and her pussy—I can do the math from there) and who do I think she is? The words wash over me because I'm stuck on a visual of her in those pretty new panties that's way better than the words she throws at me.

I've spent five years earning the respect of my club. Before that, I earned the respect of the men in my SEAL team. I don't expect her to give me anything, but I do demand a chance. I set my glass down and interrupt the flow of talk.

"What's a guy got to do to have a chance with you?"

She blinks and fidgets with her glass. "You really want to date me?"

She actually looks surprised. Maybe we're both new to the dating game? Because that would actually be fucking awesome. We could make up our own rules.

"Yeah," I say gruffly. "I sure do."

She waves a hand and I'm goddamned lucky it's the empty one. "We're completely incompatible."

I give her a slow smile because I sure as hell remember what went on between us. "Not everywhere. You like some things about me."

"That's just sex." The cutest pink blush paints her cheeks.

"You fucking love dirty sex." *Truth.*

She volleys right back.

"Which doesn't mean I love *you*."

"I don't need that." Love is on my personal no-fly list, remember? Evie developing feelings for me—other than the jump-my-bones kind—would be downright inconvenient. "Let's date. Have some fun."

"Have sex." Now she sounds completely disgruntled.

*Fuck, yeah.*

I cup her bare knee with my hand. Her skin is warm and soft, and she jumps ever so slightly when I skim my thumb over the vulnerable curve. "Sex works for me."

"There are rules for dating," she says firmly. "You don't like rules."

"What if I played by your rules?"

She stares at me like that's the craziest idea ever. "You can't play by the rules."

"Why not?" I settle back in my seat, stretching my legs out. My legs bump hers, and so far, this is pretty freaking awesome. "Tell me the rules."

She makes a face. "So you can break them?"

"Hit me." I've so got this. Doesn't matter if I'm a dating virgin—she's gonna spell it all out.

She leans forward and picks up my hand. "Five rules."

I can work with that number. Club bylaws are larger.

"First rule?" She folds down my thumb. "I won't cry about you. You don't get to make me feel bad. If you piss me off, I tell you."

No fucking way I *want* to make her cry. "You've been dating the wrong guys, princess. I can work with that, as long as you show me some respect in front of the club. You want to tear into my ass, you do it when we're alone."

Her fingers skim up the length of my index finger as if it's my dick, pinching the tip lightly. "I do 40 percent of the dating work. You do the other 60. This is not a partnership, nor is it a dictatorship."

I curl my finger around hers. "I chase you. Got it."

She tucks my index finger into my palm and tugs on my middle finger. "Three? You pick me up and we go out. If we do this, I'm not your booty call. You don't come over to my place and I don't go to yours until we have a relationship."

I can work with that, too, although celibacy is definitely not my first choice. Don't think it's hers, either.

But it's up to me to earn a repeat in her bed, and I'm good with that. Anything I've put my mind to, it's come to me.

"Four. You plan ahead if you want to see me. You don't just text or show up."

"You're gonna have to forgive me for today." I lift her hand to my mouth and press a kiss against her fingertips. "Since I didn't have the rulebook."

She goes for the kill. "And we're not having sex on the first date. Maybe not the second. If it happens again, it's because I feel close to you."

She wants the whole enchilada. Dating, a relationship, emotional intimacy. And *then* maybe she tosses me the sexual cherry and we get around to having hot, dirty sex. Sex is the epilogue in her book, when in mine it's all of the chapters except for the afterword where we say our goodbyes and head in opposite directions. Still, the only hard and fast *rule* I'm hearing is the not-on-the-first-date thing. After that? Everything is fucking negotiable.

"And then what?"

She shrugs. "And then we see what happens. Maybe we have sex. Or a relationship. Maybe we head in different directions and it's over."

"Then we've got a deal. I'm playing by your rules and you're giving me a chance."

# CHAPTER NINE

*Rev*

MY PRINCESS MAY be unavailable for sexcapades—
which is fucking a-okay with me because I'm all for
the slow build if that gets her hot—but I have one of
the old ladies from the MC book a birthday party for
the coming weekend. I figure this falls under the plan-
in-advance rule in the Evie Rulebook and since Mary
Jane's two girls are four and six, she's perfectly happy
to have me spring for some Saturday entertainment.

Tío, her old man and my club brother, has ten years
on me. His last tour of duty screwed with his head—I
like to think Mary Jane's his goddamned reward because finding an old lady like her is like hitting the
rolling jackpot at the casino. Boom—you're richer
than fucking Midas himself because you plugged your
lucky quarter into the right slot at the right moment.
Tío deserves every second of his good fortune.

I'd hung around while Mary Jane made the call, in
case she needed an assist, but she handled the party
details like a pro. Evie sounded way too perky. It's not

like I want her *un*happy, but I wouldn't have minded her sounding lonely or like she needed something. Then I could have headed on over to her place and offered to help her. Rub her back. Fix some shit. Be the fucking boyfriend of her dreams.

That was such a strange thought that I'd done my best to forget about it the entire four days until the party. I ensured a prospect kept watch over her from a nice, discreet distance and I took my turn. Not gonna ask them to do what I won't do. The Colombians were no-shows, and let me tell you, Evie leads a really boring life. The woman does nothing but work. Not like I want to see her partying and getting it on with some random stranger (because then I'd have to fucking kill him), but it can't be good for her.

Mary Jane and Tío have a two-story house with a pool about a mile from the clubhouse. One of those home security system signs is stuck in the front yard, but the real deterrent are the bikes. One look and anyone with eyes in his head knows not to mess with their house. Since Mary Jane had promised her girlfriends would pony up enough kids for a bona fide party, I'd sent over a prospect with a big-ass cake and balloons. I figured that covered all the party bases.

When the Princess Mobile pulls up, I can practically feel Evie taking in the bikes crowding the driveway. The engine keeps right on running as she peeks left, then right. Fucking looks up, too, as if she expects someone big, bad and dangerous to land on the roof of the monstrosity she drives. I whip out my phone and send her a quick text.

ME: Didn't think you were chicken.

The pause is long enough that I start to worry she might actually bail, leaving me alone with a dozen tutu-sporting, tiara-wearing little girls, when she finally responds.

EVIE: You got kids? Bcz...dating no no

If I had a kid, I'd never fuck around on the side.

ME: Kids belong to Tío's old lady

EVIE: Tío's a busy man

ME: Got some loaner kids along for the ride

EVIE: How come you're here?

ME: Cake and a beautiful woman? Come on out and make my day

I can imagine her rolling her eyes at that one. Still, she and a couple of princess chicks emerge. Mary Jane bustles out before things get too awkward, so I owe the woman. She sends Princesses Two and Three into the backyard where, she warns, *the hordes are getting restless.* No clue why we don't let women patch into the MC—they're bloodthirsty enough.

Evie kind of flutters on the walk like she's not sure

what to do—bet that pisses her off. Since I'm working on my boyfriend skills, I help her out.

"Good to see you." I brush a kiss over her cheek, same as I would for Mary Jane except for the way my dick waves a greeting of its own. "See? I planned ahead."

# CHAPTER TEN

*Eve*

LITTLE KIDS DON'T bottle their feelings up. When the five-year-old girl spots me from the doorway, tiara twinkling in the scorching sunlight, her eyes go wide and a grin splits her face. I'm pink, I sparkle and I'm there for *her*. That's all it takes.

Princesses rock. Yes, I read all those magazines by the supermarket checkout counter. I got up early to watch Kate and Will tie the knot and once upon a time I knew precisely how many unmarried princes were running around Europe in expensive sports cars and designer wear. I watched brides emerge from medieval churches, all big smiles because they'd landed their princes and were about to get on with the happily-ever-after part of the fairy tale.

I don't really want a prince. I don't need to be a princess either, although pretending's fun. The last ten years taught me how to take care of myself, and more importantly, Rocker. Independence is worth more than any crown of diamonds. Still, the way Mary Jane looks at her husband makes me think of princes and endless, public, fairy-tale kisses shared with princesses.

Sort of.

Because Tío is no prince.

He's a biker.

He's also big, his ratty T-shirt promoting a second-rate rock band that will still be playing Vegas lounges when his daughter's friends are old enough to drink legally. But he listens when his wife talks. He brings her a cupcake and a beer. He runs his hand down her hair, her arms, her back, and yes, her butt. He can't get enough of her and he's clearly anticipating the moment we all get the hell out of his yard and he can take her inside and show her how much he cares.

Exhibit A? He calls her *pumpkin* and plants a big, smacking kiss on her cheek before stepping out to take a call.

"Wow." Samantha watches him go. "You think he's for real?"

Yes. Yes, I do. Mary Jane has that look in her eye. It's part satisfaction, part happiness, and part keep-your-hands-and-your-eyes-off-my-man. She knows she's got a keeper and no one's making a move on him. Between the diamond bands on Mary Jane's ring finger and Tío's leather vest with its Hard Riders patch, her Tío is safe. I need no more bikers in my life, thank you very much.

Instead, I focus on making today's party the best party ever. It's the secret to my success. I treat each birthday like it's my first and best party ever, and whichever little girl (or boy) is birthday queen receives my undivided attention. I perform. I sing, I dance and I kill the dragon.

Afterward, while party guests scream and mainline cake, I pack up my props. The house is gorgeous, the kind of place I've secretly dreamed of owning years in the future. Mary Jane's kid is cute and her husband hot. I'm just not sure where or how the MC factors in. I didn't even know bikers bought real estate that wasn't a dive bar, pawnshop, or some other seedy enterprise. The bikers I've known had addresses like Lovelock Correctional Center and Ely State Prison.

Mary Jane hums off-key as she saunters up to me to hand me an envelope of cash. "Thanks for making my daughter's day."

"You're welcome." If I had my way, every kid who wanted a princess party would get one, too. I'd spend my waking hours in tiaras and tulle.

Mary Jane's silent for a moment and I try playing it cool—but we're both staring at Tío and Rev. Sprawled in lawn chairs on the opposite side of the stamped concrete patio, they hold longnecks and watch the kids' antics like there's nowhere they'd rather be. I've always assumed bikerly debauches involve adult women, kegs and salacious X-rated activities, but they seem to be having a good time.

"They're great guys," Mary Jane says with a little sigh.

"Uh-huh." I pack my shit faster. Rev's a gorgeous guy, and I'd have to be blind not to notice. My libido wakes up when he's around and it's easy to forget he's a biker and a badass watching him listen intently to a five-year-girl explaining why purple is her favorite color. And another part of my anatomy stirs when he announces that *his* favorite color is blue. I'm sure he's just being polite (although Rev is one of the *least* polite people I've met), but the girl nods and runs off happily. I like that he listened. That it didn't matter to him that she wasn't discussing the fate of the nation or the tanking economy or supersecret biker stuff. He listened. He volunteered a few words of his own.

Hell, I like blue, too.

He stands up, so I stare some more. The man has legs that deserve to be looked at. The faded denim of his jeans tightens with each step he takes—and I'd like to start at the bottom and work my way up. When he stops in front of me, I'm still staring. He plucks the plastic box of props out of my arms and aims a crooked grin at me that should be illegal. Hell, the entire man is a walking felony.

He tips his head at the box. "Where to?"

The question would be easier to answer if I stopped staring. His eyes are warm and heated, a dark brown reminding me of my favorite things. Chocolate. This great faux-fur blanket I bought for my house. Puppy dogs and cowboy boots. I bet he'd taste as good, too. Bet he'd feel—

"Evie?" He sounds amused.

"Yeah?"

"You wanna tell me where to put this?" He hefts the container higher in his arms, in case I need the visual. Which I totally do. I'm staring at the man like I've been on a no-carbs diet for a week and he's the world's biggest, sweetest, tastiest doughnut ever. I'm pretty sure I'm drooling.

It's not my fault his package is so appealing.

"The RV," I blurt out.

"Uh-huh." He shoots me that crooked half grin again, as if he can see the X-rated party taking place in my head. He brushes past me, his arm rubbing some very non-PG areas. I follow because he's got my stuff and I have questions.

"Why are you really here?"

Behind us come the sounds of Mary Jane wrapping up the party. He opens the door to the RV and steps inside. This is the point where I'd like to pretend I stop following him and do something strong and independent. It's not like I want or need to knee him in the balls to assert my ability to stand on my own two feet, but he's just so effortlessly in control that it grates. I hesitate, but he disappears inside my RV and I'm not done talking with him. To him. Fuck if I know what I'm really doing here, other than going in after him.

I step inside.

"Where does this go?" He hefts the box. There's not much space inside the RV. In addition to the built-in table and benches, there's a bed, a tiny bathroom and a galley kitchen consisting of a Mr. Coffee, a toaster oven and a mini-fridge whose capacity maxes out at a six-pack.

"On the bed. Why are you really here today?"

He deposits the box and turns around, reminding me the RV's short on space. Without even trying, the man consumes every inch and then some. He's even bigger than Mary Jane's Tío and the way his shoulders brush the wall just calls attention (my attention) to his body.

He shrugs. "You made the rules."

Words blah blah words. I fight the urge to step forward and run my hands up that big, broad chest.

"About?"

He looks at me like he's never been more serious in his life. "Dating."

"And you're playing by my rules?" Hello. It's hard to imagine Rev putting the brakes on anything at my say-so.

"I'm giving it a shot, princess. The way I see it, if I hang out here with you, I can keep an eye out for the Colombians. They're not gonna give a shit that you're a civvie in this war."

"So you're here entirely as my bodyguard? To protect me?" I take a moment to imagine Rev as my bodyguard, pressing me beneath or behind his big body at the first hint of danger. Taking the Colombian business seriously is hard because I'm not sure I've ever met somebody from Colombia, let alone a somebody who engages in illegal drug-running and wants to maim or kill me. The only danger right now is to my panties and that's all Rev's fault.

"Entirely?" He looks amused. "Let's give it 30 percent, okay?"

"I only merit a 30 percent effort?"

"No." The man *moves*. God, he has great moves. He closes the space between us in two steps that are part swagger, part prowl, and that's not even the best part. Nope. The RV is so small that now he's pressed against me. He threads his fingers through mine (I'm in no mood to resist) and draws my hands over my head with one of his. Pretty sure he notices the shiver that rocks me with *that* move.

"Ask me about the other 70 percent," he whispers, mouth against my ear. "Ask *nicely*."

Holy. *Shit*.

True confession time. "I'm not sure I'm capable of conversation right now."

His free hand finds my hip and his mouth moves over my ear—is he tasting me? Whatever he's doing, I'm melting. "Thirty percent for the fucking Colombians because I promised to keep you safe and I never break a promise. The other 70 percent is my favorite part, though. You said I was supposed to chase you. You made it a fucking rule, babe."

"Those were dating rules," I protest. Not hard, mind you, because who wouldn't enjoy this?

"This was a party. You're dressed up. There's beer and good times. Sounds date-worthy to me."

The party's over but—details. I thread my fingers through his. We fit together, our fingers meshing like we've done this a million times before.

Like we really do belong together.

"Do you want it to count?"

"If we were on a date, I'd want to kiss you good-night."

"Are you asking me if I kiss on the first date?"

We've had dirty sex, but we haven't had a date. Rev's crooked grin reaches his eyes and makes me want to smile back. To nod my head and agree wholeheartedly with whatever he proposes. I can't think when I'm around him—all I do is feel.

Feel wonderful.

Alive.

On fire for him.

He runs a finger over my bottom lip and I feel his touch everywhere, from my mouth to my pussy to parts in between that feel suspiciously like my heart.

He's the best kind of trouble, his fingers exploring my mouth, leaving shivers and heat where he touches. He doesn't push, doesn't hurry. Just takes his time as if we have hours, days, just plain forever to kiss.

He sucks my finger into his mouth, his tongue exploring my skin. Licking, teasing, coaxing me into relaxing and letting go because the feelings fill me up until I forget where we are and all the reasons to slow this thing down still further.

When he nips my bottom lip, I catch his lower lip between my own teeth and bite right back. Harder. The sensations threaten to drown me, sweeping over me in bright, hot waves of pleasure. He kisses me and kisses me, like he doesn't want to lose the contact either, taking and then taking more. His hand settles on my thighs, his palms easing upward beneath my dress.

And then he stops because, clearly, the man is a born tease. He turns his face until his cheek rests against mine, his face buried in my hair.

"Go out with me." I feel his question on my skin.

"Kiss me again," I counter.

"Answer first." He gives orders, but he also gives me what I need.

He covers my mouth with his, his tongue parting my lips. The sweetest of pressures and he's in, his tongue stroking mine as he goes as deep as he can. He tastes like the vanilla from the cupcake frosting he stole, like chocolate and all the things I shouldn't crave. He's a wild, wicked flavor, a million guilty calories and midnight cravings, and I won't say no. This is just a kiss, but Rev is someone special. I can't help but recognize the truth even as he slants his mouth deeper, taking more.

When he lifts his head, my fingers are digging into his shoulders. He's not close enough.

"You got an answer for me, princess?"

"Remind me of the question."

A look of smug contentment flashes over his face. He's earned it.

"Go out with me for real." He cups my face in his hands and rests his forehead against mine. "Fucking dying here, Evie, so help me out."

He's never asked me for anything before. Told, yes. Ordered, absolutely. But asked? Never. I can't help but wonder if he knows his thumb is stroking my skin.

"One date," he says. "A dozen. You don't have to like me. Fuck, you don't have to put out again. I just want the time. With you."

The lost look in his eyes makes something inside me turn over.

"Yes," I say, because I like that look. I like *him*.

# CHAPTER ELEVEN

*Eve*

YOU KNOW WHEN you're having a nightmare? How you try to wake yourself up and point out all the reasons to your sleeping self that the shit unfolding around you is dream rather than reality? And in the dream, you start by pinching and poking, and then you escalate to just standing there in front of the train or the psycho killer or whatever it is that's trying to kill you? That's kind of how my week goes. It's a blur of birthday parties and business meetings, of increasingly demanding phone calls to ever-louder radio silence from Rocker. That's the nightmare.

But then there are the really sweet, also-can't-be-real moments where Rev flexes his dating muscle. He's always riding past or in the neighborhood when I'm out. He's sticking to his promise to look out for me, and that's more annoying-cute than anything. But we also go for coffee and I tease him about the barista checking him out. We spend an evening playing penny lines at a casino on the Strip, me perched on his lap as we fed the coins in together. When we win five bucks, Rev calls me his good luck charm and shares the luck—and the five bucks—with a homeless veteran panhandling outside. He gives good date—and he doesn't rush me.

The moments in between our dates and work are trickier, leaving way too much time for worrying about Rocker. I tell myself Rocker probably believes he has reasons for networking with the Colombian cartel. God, I hate even thinking about him as a drug dealer. Because if he's selling drugs or in any way making it possible, he's not *just* my little brother anymore. He's a drug dealer.

Since Rev's accusations and my own suspicions aren't indisputable fact, I reach out to Rocker. And yes, this means I call and text him in every free moment. I can tell from my phone when Rocker's seen my texts, but he only answers one in ten. Tonight is apparently one of those buy-a-lottery-ticket exceptions and God's in a good mood or looking out for big sisters, because when I look down at my phone, the line of bouncing dots means Rocker is typing.

ROCKER: Where you at?

ME: Home. We need to talk.

ROCKER: You okay?

ME: Dating a friend of yours

ROCKER: ?

ME: Try reading yr messages. Seeing yr friend Rev.

I use the long pause that follows to shimmy into my
pajamas. I might want to do some preemptive shopping before any sleepovers with Rev. My usual night-
wear is a pair of yoga pants and an old University of
Nevada T-shirt. Not precisely Sexyville and the man
clearly likes his Victoria's Secret.

I try the T-shirt without the pants, but that doesn't
send the right message, either. I've been hesitant to tap
Rev's present, but I own no date-worthy underwear.
My panties go under princess party dresses—and princesses are good girls.

Eventually my phone buzzes again.

ROCKER: Not xctly friends.

ME: Give me more words.

ROCKER: Different club, k? And your boy's trouble. Works as club enforcer. So keep your eyes open.
Lemme know what you see. Inside intel on the MC
good.

ME: WTF? I look like Mata Hari to you?

ROCKER: Got some serious shit going down. Need
to know you're safe.

ME: You are a pain in my ass.

ROCKER: Love you. Do it for me?

ME: Love you too. Lemme know when you have time to talk?

The roar of a Harley pulling into my driveway has never been so welcome. I need answers from Rocker, but I'm not sure I really want them. If everything was fine, if he wasn't doing something he knew would worry me, he'd tease me about treating him like he's five. He'd laugh, but he'd make sure I stopped worrying. Rocker's good like that.

He's what family should be.

We have each other's back and we do it with love. No matter what's happened or going down or screwed up, we love each other. That's the ultimate rule and neither of us has ever broken it. Why would we? Love isn't something you turn on or off.

My phone buzzes again. This time, when I look down this time, I'll have answers. Everything will be okay and I'll go out front, get on Rev's bike and tell him he was wrong about Rocker. Power of positive thinking for the win. But when I look down, I've got just one word.

ROCKER: Later

# CHAPTER TWELVE

*Rev*

WHEN I PULL UP for our date, Evie flies out the door of her house. I swing off my bike and intercept her coming down the path. Pretty sure that's in the dating rulebook, but I just want an excuse to put my hands on her. Her jeans hug her ass and legs, the faded denim disappearing into a pair of boots that are perfect spank bank material. They lace up her calves, the tall heel giving her step a sexy swing. The fitted pink T-shirt cupping her tits is even better, as is the ponytail I could fist while I drill into her. Hold her still for my kiss.

Christ.

I'm supposed to be dating her, not mentally stripping her on the sidewalk.

"Hey." I cup her elbows, drawing her close. Brush a kiss over her mouth.

"Rev." Her smile makes me feel like I just won gold in the world's biggest competition. I do a quick sanity check, and spot the brown leather jacket dangling from her fingers. Good. Don't want her getting chewed up on the road.

"Come on." I curl my fingers around hers and tug her toward my bike. Even as a preacher's kid, I got more than my share of girls growing up, but we weren't in it for the long haul. I was the king of fun and sex, but that was as far as it went. Kind of like taking the bike from one side of town to the other, when this thing with Evie is more long-distance haul, the best kind of ride on the highway where I can open it up and just ride wherever the road leads.

I pop a helmet on her head and straddle the bike. She swings on behind me like she's been doing that all her life. Her legs grip my hips, her pussy tucked against my ass. She slides her arms around my stomach, linking her fingers just above my belt buckle. Heading back inside her place sounds better and better. Instead, I take us to the Strip. Figure she's never ridden down it on the back of a bike.

First time I've ever been glad for traffic, too. The Strip's jammed with cars and those vans with the twelve-foot dirty pictures of women inviting guys to call now for the ultimate party. Surprised the T&A display doesn't cause more accidents, frankly. When the lights change, we wait for the crowds of sightseeing, gambling, drunk-ass people to cross.

She admires the view and I admire her. Figure it's a fair trade. Whenever she shifts to look at something new, her tits skim my back. You know those little brush things percussionists use on their cymbals? She plays me just like that. Each time I feel Evie against me, soft and gentle, I get harder and the urge to toss all my plans—for protecting her and the club's interests—grows stronger. I mean, fuck—we're surrounded by hotels with rooms for rent. Not like I'm not gonna get ideas about Evie, a bed and a few hours of alone time.

But that's not what she wants. I mean, I could talk her into it. Slide my hand back between us and stroke her through her jeans until she's squirming and begging for it. Evie's hot and she's lonely. It would feel really good too until it was over. And then what? Shit would get awkward.

She makes another happy noise and does more squirming. My dick's about to bust out of my jeans, so I look around, desperate for a distraction. We're idling in traffic right in front of Paris Las Vegas. Not content with little French bistros, the developers decided to recreate the entire Eiffel Tower. It soars above us like some big French dick. At night, it's lit up and the view from the top rocks. Went up there once and watched the fountains at the Bellagio shoot off.

"You ever been to France?" That's me. King of the fucking small talk.

I feel her shake her head. "I'd like to go. And you?"

"Never." I fight the urge to head straight to the airport. Airlines never fill all of their seats. Bet we could be on a flight headed to France before tomorrow. Instead, I take us out to Red Rock. They've got a thirteen-mile scenic drive that I think she'll like. It's not the most romantic shit in the world, but riding's who I am. It's what I do.

We spend a couple of hours exploring the rock formations. The sun goes down late in the summer, so we've still got more shadows than dark when we head back. Although the road's been more or less empty the last hour or so, there's an SUV coming up fast behind us now, one of those big, black numbers you see in the movies or in the hands of the Feds. Probably just some suburban wannabe who likes driving the biggest goddamned thing in the parking lot, but I don't like its speed. I consider pulling my gun, but this is my fucking date. Reaching between us to grab my piece won't endear me to Evie. So I ride, watching our company in my mirror.

The SUV gains.

I could cut across the sand right now, but that's not a smooth ride.

"Think we might have company," I tell her.

Of course she twists, scouting for trouble. Bastards know we know they're there now. The SUV responds by accelerating until they're riding my ass. Don't think they're actually out for blood, because we're an easy target out here. Question is what they do want.

That's when the second SUV crests a small rise in the road in front of us. Fuck. That's not good. Looks like they have a plan after all. I should have kept the club's eyes on Evie, but I wanted this date with her. Didn't want to share her, but full coverage would have been good now.

"Shit may get rocky," I warn her. "Need you to hang on tight and do whatever I say, you hear me? Not the time for any independent bullshit."

God bless her, Evie threads her fingers through my belt and her grip on my legs tightens.

Thirty seconds later, the first shot rings out, kicking up gravel two feet to the right of the bike. Evie screams a curse into my ear and her hands almost cut me in half. Good girl.

In order to fire back, I'll have to slow down, reach behind me and free my piece. Not like it's rocket science, but I don't know how Evie's gonna react. I'm licensed to conceal-carry, but there's some shit we haven't talked about yet. Right now, my safest bet is to ride like hell and get her under cover. I double-check the fuel tank, but it's not a long ride—just a hard one.

The fuckers in the SUV behind us pop off another series of shots. Can't tell if they're missing on purpose or just that bad.

"Hold on," I bark and hang a hard right. We fly off the road, the bike's front end slamming down into a sand wash. I throttle back as much as I can because the desert's not a hospitality suite and a flat tire or a hidden rock now would kill us. Hell, a tip-over wouldn't be better—the shooter could pick us off from the shoulder. The scenery snaps past us in a wild rush, sand kicking up as we tear through the mesquite. Low-hanging branches slap at us as I weave through the rough, aiming for the rocky canyons. As soon as we're under cover, I kill the motor. Highway's a good mile behind us, and it's practically silent.

Evie hasn't let go once.

I reach around between us and slip my gun free.

I scoop her up and drag her into my lap. "You okay?"

Since I really need to know the answer to that, seems like the right place to start.

"No." She makes a little hiccupping sound. Shit. Is she crying? I don't want to take my eyes off the road, because those SUV-driving bastards may be coming after us, but is she hurt? I didn't feel her take a hit, but anything's possible.

Fuck it.

"Where are you hurt?" I pat her down, not waiting for her answer. She looks fine. No visible entrance or exit wounds. No blood. She's just pale, those god-damned tears spilling down her cheeks and punching a hole in me.

"Somebody tried to kill us."

In her nice, safe, normal world, people don't gun for other people. They probably say please and thank you all the time, too, go to church on Sundays and feed the homeless. My world—Rocker's world—is different.

She burrows her face into my chest and I ignore the spreading damp patch. The SUV's stopped on the shoulder. Nobody gets out, however, and a couple of minutes later, it pulls back onto the highway, headed toward Vegas.

Thank fuck when she lifts her head, she's not crying anymore. "Were those Colombians?"

Since no one stopped and made introductions, there's no way to know. It's entirely possible that her fuckwit brother has pissed off multiple groups of people—or that they were gunning for me.

"Definite possibility," I bite out before I can lift her off the bike, take her to the ground and get inside her.

We're in the desert, for Christ's sake, and shit's happened that she's upset about. I should not be thinking about pushing her shirt up, her jeans down, and ripping her panties off.

I'm a biker, not a fucking psychologist. Evie's face twists and she bites down on her lower lip hard enough to bleed. Hearing your shit's gone south isn't good news, so there's probably something else I'm supposed to say here, but all I can think is what the fuck was Rocker thinking? Her brother should have known this would hurt her. All I can do is pat her back like an idiot, making sure my body's between hers and anyone coming at us.

"Pretty sure that was someone making a point. I think we should head back," I say slowly. Don't want to scare her more, but we're not in a great position here. I text my president because he needs to know what's up. Hawke promises to send some brothers to check out Evie's place. Good. No point in riding into an ambush. I fire off a couple more texts while I'm at it, because you can never have too much security.

"What did Rocker get himself into?"

We've gone over this once before, but she wasn't ready to listen. Now, she is. That's the power of show-and-tell for you, ladies and gentlemen.

"Bad shit." I shrug. "Moving product isn't the safest thing, but there are better and worse ways to do it. He's definitely picked the worse way."

Too blunt? Too bad. Lying gets people killed and she deserves the truth.

"There's no way for you to get him out of this?" She

stares at me as if I'm some kind of superhero, and for her, I'd like to be.

"Not sure," I admit. "Gonna find out for you, okay? Just give me a little time, Evie."

"He might die," she says way too softly.

Not much I can say, because it's the truth. Her brother has a goddamned death wish.

# CHAPTER THIRTEEN

*Eve*

I'VE NEVER LIKED a side of danger with my sex. But by
the time Rev and I reach my house, the fear has become
something else. Getting shot at tops no foreplay list
I've read, but I'm turned on. Or maybe it's my safety-
seeking instinct, my hormones certain that hooking up
with the man mountain in front of me would be wise
in light of my Colombian situation. Or maybe I'm just
looking for excuses.

Rev moves fast for such a big man. He has me off
the bike, up the sidewalk and at the door before I can
say anything. When I unlock it, he's so close that my
butt brushes his front.

"I'm gonna come by and install a security system
tomorrow," he tells me. "Should have done it before,
but didn't want to freak you out. I've got a couple
of prospects watching over you, too, and I've texted
Rocker so he knows there's a problem."

"Rev?"

"Yeah?"

"Shut up." I tug him inside.

Grabbing a bottle of wine from the counter, I head for the fireplace. I don't give a shit it's summer. I turn on the gas low, letting the flames lick up the logs. When Rev turns away from the door, the gun tucked in the waistband of his jeans is a visual reminder that he's a biker and not a nice guy.

"Is being in the club always like that?"

He gives me a hard look. "Got to admit, today's not been a winner."

"Help me fix that?" Yes. I'm breaking all my rules. I take a long drink from the bottle and set it down on the floor. Lay down on my stomach watching the flames flicker on the ceramic logs in the fireplace.

"No do-overs in life, princess." I wouldn't take the option anyhow. My choices have led me straight here to him and losing him isn't something I can imagine right now. He's the best kind of all wrong. So when he drops onto the rug beside me, stretching his legs out? Screw it. Tonight, I'm all in. All about living and feeling, make-believing everything's going to be a-okay.

I roll over, straddling his legs as I reach for his belt. I pause for a brief second to appreciate the impressive bulge and then, fingers flying, I undo the buckle. His buttons pop, one after another. The dark cotton of his boxer briefs is the tissue paper inside the box of the best Christmas present ever. God, the man's built. I skim my hands up the outline of his dick to where the tip juts above the edge of his boxers. He makes me feel so much.

He grabs the bottle and steals a swallow of wine. "This really what you want, babe?"

I want him so much that I have no words.

"Less talking, more doing," I whisper and pull his jeans down his body. Seconds later his boots are off, followed by his shirt. I told Rev to take things slow because I needed to make sure sex with him was the right thing to do, but getting shot at changes everything. Rev feels good, neither of us is dead, and those are the only priorities that matter. Foreplay and patience aren't necessary because I just want him in me now. Plus, his dick's a work of art. He jerks when I run a finger up his thick erection. Time to make shit perfectly clear.

"That's mine," I tell him.

"You think?" He sounds amused.

"Possession's nine-tenths of the law." Leaning forward, I suck him into my mouth.

"Jesus Christ." He falls back on his elbows, big hands tangling in my hair. His dick goes from zero to sixty, the thick head pushing at the back of my throat. I relax and take him deeper, savoring his harsh groan.

Right now, he's all mine.

*Rev*

Evie sucks me like a pro, making me the luckiest fucking man alive. When she said she wasn't putting out until we had a relationship going, I agreed to respect her boundaries. Not sure how that translated into a blowjob, but when her lips close around my dick, my hips shoot off the floor.

So much for slow. I'm about to come in her mouth and that's way too fast for both of us. I've had women go down on me, but this is different. This is the best.

This is my Evie.

She sucks harder, lips moving up and down my dick like I'm her favorite flavor and my balls tighten. Fuck, she's good. The best kind of dirty bad. I'm supposed to make sure of her because she's the club's ace in the hole, but how do I turn down this? I fist her hair, guiding her deeper and lower. Makes me even more of a bastard—I know that.

I tug her face away from my dick when we get way too close to the point of no return. "You want to do this? No more waiting?"

Her face turns pink and not from the fire. She bites her lip, momentarily uncertain, then her face turns fierce. "Yes."

*Green fucking light.*

I roll her onto her back, desperate to get her naked. Her clothes go flying. Shirt, jeans, bra, panties. Thank Christ she lost her shoes somewhere between the front door and the fire, because otherwise I'd be slamming into her half-dressed.

Not gonna lie—eating Evie out is my all-time favorite. Who knew ten minutes could be a fucking lifetime highlight? I stretch my time, licking and teasing, plumping her tits in my hand and pinching the nipples when I stop playing and let go. I'm supposed to give it to her slow, but I always ride balls-out on the highway.

Really hope her curtains aren't for shit because her neighbors are about to get a show. Kneeing her legs apart, I make a place for myself. She bucks up against me. Nope, nothing slow about this at all. My dick is hard as a rock, and I need to be inside her. She's on the same page because she tilts her hips up.

Engraved invitation right there.

I yank her legs over my thighs and sit back. World's best view ever. The fire's heat plays over her bare skin, lighting up her eyes. Her hair goes every which way and her pussy's slick and wet.

*Mine.*

I find her clit, circling her with my thumb. God-damned beautiful. She's soaking wet, which will make this easier.

"You want to fuck any particular way?"

She whimpers something, eyes closing, but the sounds coming out of her mouth make no sense. Guess that means it's my turn to choose.

I stroke my fingers up and down, dipping deeper into her pussy with each pass. When my thumb rubs her clit, she breathes faster and faster. I'm trying to be sweet and slow, to check all the boxes on her list. It's not me, this nice guy, but for Evie I'll give it a shot.

"Now," she gasps. "How about now?"

Now sure works for me. I won't last long once I'm in her. I tear the condom open, rolling the rubber down in record time. I want her bare, but I won't make her feel unsafe.

As she whimpers and clenches beneath me, work-ing her way toward her own orgasm, I shove her legs farther apart. I want her to come *for* me, on me, because I'm the man who does it for her and she trusts me to give her nothing but pleasure. Yeah, I know life doesn't work that way, but reality's taking a temporary vacation.

I set my dick against her and push inside. I'm big, she's small, and so it's slow going. She's tight and her pussy grips me like she's never letting go, but when I thrust harder, she rewards me with a moan.

"Relax," I grunt against her ear. She's gotta open up and let me in. When she squirms, trying to take me, I pin her in place. Makes me a fucking Neanderthal, but I thread my fingers through hers and draw her hands over her head so I'm in control.

She finally relaxes beneath me when I find her clit with my free hand.

"Fast or slow?"

"Fast," she groans. I slam into her, riding her hard, and it feels so damned good. I finger her clit, stroking her with each downward thrust, and she more than meets me. And when she clenches around me, gasping and shrieking, that's my name on her lips.

Best. Sound. Ever.

I drive into her, holding her hips and thrusting faster and faster. Giving her the words because she gets everything I've got. "You're fucking gorgeous."

She collapses beneath me as she comes, clutching me with her arms and legs, and I flip her around, drilling into her from behind. I wrap her ponytail around my wrist, pulling her head back for my kiss.

"Make me forget," she whispers, and I wonder if it's

possible to come apart with all these feelings coming alive inside me. The pleasure rockets through me and I come fast and dirty, slamming into her once, twice, three times. She whimpers and relaxes as if there's no more anything left in her.

And yeah, I'm smiling against her throat. Might not move for the next couple of hours. Might be days. Rolling onto my side, I wrap an arm around her waist and haul her against me. She wriggles, but I'm not letting go now.

"We should get up," she announces.

"Enjoy the moment, princess."

I tangle one hand in her hair, playing with the silky strands. Who fucking knew I could cuddle? It's nice, though. Kinda like the two of us just lying here together.

"We're going to make a mess on the rug." She makes another bid for freedom. "And you probably need to get going."

"You're really not one for afterglow, are you?"

"Is that a problem?" The grumpy in her voice makes me smile.

"Might want to give it a shot. See what you think," I suggest. "And let me worry about any mess. I got this."

She must agree with me because she yawns, and next thing I know, she's drifting off to sleep.

# CHAPTER FOURTEEN

*Eve*

THE MAN SCREWED me into a coma. This must be why I wake up in bed.

Alone. And naked.

I never noticed when he picked me up and moved me in the middle of the night. Forget melatonin—Rev is a one-man testament to the superior sleeping power of a good orgasm. I grab a quick shower, pull on some clothes and stagger out to the kitchen in search of coffee. Rev's passed out on my couch. Sprawled on his back, he looks bigger than ever, which has to be impossible. Heat flushes my body as I take in his relaxed form. His legs are bent, one arm thrown over his head. *Boyfriend* is such a weird word. I try it silently, not quite ready to say it out loud. *My boyfriend, Rev.* Or maybe *this is* my *boyfriend.* So what if he rocks my world sexually? It does *not* mean I canonize him.

He certainly doesn't look saintlike. Saints absolutely do not come with broad shoulders or such powerful biceps. Tattoos are also definitely not saintly accessories. I don't own a single throw pillow—he can't possibly be comfortable. Instead of worrying about the man's comfort, however, I'm helplessly focused on the way his T-shirt rides up, exposing his stomach and six-pack abs. How does he manage to take up all the space in my house?

"Feel free to touch," he rumbles, eyes still closed. "Or you just gonna stand there?"

I reach for him, trailing my fingers over that tempting strip of skin. God. He's hard and silky, heated and so impossibly, wonderfully male. Or maybe that's thanks to the impossible-to-ignore ridge beneath the worn denim clinging to his body. Denim. My favorite kind of gift-wrapping.

"My bed had room for two," I whisper.

"I have a hard time sleeping with other people around." He opens his eyes.

Calloused fingers wrap around my wrist and tug gently. Funny how he reads both deadly and safe at the same time, as if he's ready to give the rest of the world a beat down but then he holds me with such care. Despite my awkward perch on the side of the couch, I go all in. I throw my leg over his hips and straddle him like I'm a cowgirl and he's my best saddle. He invited me down, so he can put up or shut up.

"Hell of a way to wake up." His smile is slow, sleepy and so fucking perfect.

"Tell me about it," I whisper back. Since I need to put my hands somewhere, I set them on his chest. The heat of him radiates through the thin T-shirt, and his musky scent teases me. Rev smells like oil and leather and danger. Like the open road and freedom. The sleepy smile transforms his face from fierce to sensually predatory, as if he's thinking about taking a bite out of me—or having himself a taste.

*Please, please taste me.*

Rev takes his time, running his thumbs over my hips, tracing the line of my bikini panties through my jeans. I fight the urge to relax into that wicked touch, leaning toward him when he doesn't move further. He just takes me in, sprawled beneath me like some great beast.

"I need to know something." The man's a mystery, but part of me feels as if I've known him for years. God. This is so bad. In the dating world, I've just cannonballed into the deep end of the pool—and the water might be way too shallow.

"Shoot," he says casually.

"What's the deal between you and my brother? Are you friends or what?"

Rocker hasn't touched base with me yet this morning and that's unusual. He usually has a sixth sense about when I'm trouble. Or bothered. Worked up about anything. For Rev, I'm all three, plus there's my SUV run-in yesterday.

"Shit's complicated." Nope. Not an answer at all.

"I'm generally not considered stupid." I don't like playing games—and I really don't want to play with Rev. Throw him down, rip his clothes off, have my way with him? Yes, yes and hell yes. Word games, however, aren't my thing.

Rev mutters an obscenity. "I'm Hard Rider. He's Black Dog. Our clubs have some differences of opinion."

"Anything I should be concerned about?"

His eyes hold mine, hardening with resolution. "Not one goddamned thing for you to worry about. You know much about club life?"

I wiggle, getting comfortable—although the impressive erection pressed against my pussy doesn't lend itself to *comfort*. "Rocker and I grew up as club rats. Our dad rode with a local club. He never made officer, but he patched in and rode with them. Helped out when they called and stuff, which didn't work out so well for us."

Rev could make a killing playing poker because I can't tell what he's thinking. His face is blank and unreadable, his eyes no longer warm and hot. Am I pissing him off by talking shit about someone else's club? I won't bullshit about this, however, because my dad's club wasn't good for our family. It ripped us apart.

"He got twenty-five to fifty for transporting weapons," I say way too loudly. "He went away and then Rocker and I bounced around after that. Our mom wasn't making much and times were tough."

"Club shoulda taken care of you," Rev growls.

"If wishes were horses, I'd be able to run the Preakness single-handed. That part of my life is over and done with, but I'm not a big club fan."

He nods, hand dipping lower. "Hear you on that. You got plans for today?"

"Work." I offer him a regretful smile.

"Be better if you stayed put today."

"For who? I have a job. Money to earn. Five-year-olds to please. No work means no cash and I've got my bills to pay."

Rev stills. It's not as if he was a sea of motion before, but something in him goes quiet as if he's working on not unleashing his inner predator. "Ask Rocker about your going into work today."

I swing off Rev's lap. Clearly, we need to work on his relationship skills before he's ready for me to make my next move, because hello? It's the twenty-first century and I don't take orders from whatever man's decorating my life at the moment. "We should be clear on one thing. Rocker's not my owner."

I look after Rocker, not the other way round.

"Fuck." Rev shoves upright, running a hand over his head. "Didn't mean to imply he was, but shit's going down."

"Rev?"

"Yeah?"

"This is where you tell me about the *shit going down* and then I make my own decision, like the big girl I am."

"If you grew up in a club, you know I can't discuss club business with you."

This isn't a battle I'm winning today, so I head for the kitchen and my BFF, Mr. Coffee. I need to leave and I'd prefer to go caffeinated. While the coffee brews, I retreat down the hall and do my princess hair and makeup. When I come back, a fully dressed Rev is by the front door, holding out a to-go mug of coffee.

"Thanks, honey," I say, rolling my eyes.

He promptly raises the cup up too high for me to reach. "Nobody's forcing you to drink it."

Since coffee is both the elixir of the gods and mandatory this early in the morning, I reach for the cup, plastering my body against his as I stretch. No point in letting him have all the fun. When my fingers close around the handle, I plant a quick, hard kiss on his gorgeous mouth. The man's lips are downright sinful, and not just because they make me think about sex. And talking dirty.

And a million other things I shouldn't do.

He grunts as I let go of his beautiful body and brush past him. My girls are waiting in my driveway.

Rev follows me outside. "Still wish you'd rethink."

"You have information to share with me?" Rocker asked me to keep my eyes and ears peeled, so I'll touch bases with him. Club business that worries Rev could touch Rocker, too. Maybe he'll benefit from the heads-up.

"Nope," he says easily, gaze moving over the pink RV.

"Bye," I say at the same moment Rev hooks a finger in the back of my jeans and tugs. I take an involuntary step backward and debate the wisdom of launching my coffee cup at his head. Bet that would piss him off and he'd do something about it. This leads to dirty thoughts about how Rev might express that displeasure, starting with his big hand on my butt. *No sexy fantasies on a workday.* Shit. I need to schedule time with my vibrator. In real life, I have zero interest in being draped over my guy's knee for a spanking, but I sure enjoy the hell out of the fantasy.

"Your brother lost the guy we had watching his ass, so change of plans. Where you go, I go. Fucking biblical."

"Ummm. What?" My childhood didn't exactly feature Bible camps, but I'm certain that Jesus Christ didn't encourage swearing, seeing as how there's a commandment specifically forbidding it.

"I'm your bodyguard," Rev announces like it makes perfect sense.

"Not sure I understand," I admit. "You've been following my brother?"

He gives me a small, hard smile. "I'm gonna stick by your side today. Tomorrow. As many days as it takes. You know that story in the Bible about Ruth?"

Uh, no. I sure don't. I'll never be one of those people name-dropping chapters and verses. Rev wraps me up in his big arms.

"Ruth hooks up with this guy. Marries him and moves in with him, which is a big deal because he's from a different country and worships different gods. He up and dies, and then it's just Ruth and her mother-in-law, Naomi."

"Is this a mother-in-law horror story?" I try and fail to imagine Rev married. He's not the kind of guy you'd spot standing at the altar in a black tux.

He shakes his head. "Ruth and Naomi are tight. Naomi's trying to convince Ruth to pack up and move back to her own country because shit's not going well for Naomi and she doesn't want to suck Ruth into her mess. They're family, they've made commitments to each other, so Ruth isn't having it."

He gives me a hard-eyed look at this. Am I supposed to be Naomi in this scenario?

"Ruth tells Naomi straight-up that Naomi's stuck with her. Where Naomi goes, Ruth goes. Where Naomi stays, Ruth stays. Ruth vows she's making Naomi's people and Naomi's gods her own."

Color me confused. He must read that truth on my face, because he sighs, and keeps talking. "When someone patches into a club, he promises the club comes first, no matter what. And I've made those promises to Hard Riders. Won't lie to you about that. But I'm making you a promise of my own—no matter how bad your situation gets, I've got your back. You count on me. I'm not free to ask you to be my old lady and wear my patch—too much shit between my club and your brother's. But if I was looking for that kind of relationship, you'd be the woman I'd be looking for."

"So I'm…Naomi?" Pretty sure my voice sounds slightly hysterical.

He nods. "And I'm sticking by you."

I think about it. Nope. I'm still confused as hell.

"Not worried about the state of my soul," he allows. "So never mind the Bible story. But I am worried about the state of your ass. It's mine and you're stuck with me. Made a promise to keep you safe, remember? Where you go, I'm going, so give me the address of today's party."

I give up trying to understand him.

"When did you read the Bible?"

He reaches around me to take the birthday party invitation Samantha silently extends from the RV. "My daddy was a pastor. Some of it stuck."

"How about we try the explanations again, but without the metaphors?"

He just looks at me. Story of my life.

"Never mind," I say. "I'm leaving. Stick or don't stick. It's your call."

# CHAPTER FIFTEEN

*Rev*

I LIKE A GIRL who's willing. Someone who takes orders in bed and prefers her sex dirty. Someone who understands the club comes first and that I'm out when my prez calls. Evie should fucking be grateful I'm bodyguarding her fine ass because the Colombians make me look like the choirboy I never was. So yeah, she should thank me.

I know something about gratitude, too. Not a day's gone by when I haven't acknowledged to myself that my club saved my ass and set me on the road I'm riding on today. At seventeen, I'd been my old man's rebel son. I'd liked sex, I'd liked sin and I'd never met a rule I didn't want to break. Shit had hit the fan the night my old man had been hit by a drunk driver, and the club had been there for me.

Gratitude is not part of Princess's repertoire. After finishing her second party, she stalks past me and into the Princess Mobile as if I'm the invisible man. I'm debating how to respond when my phone rings and caller

ID warns fun and games are over. Hawke's on the line and the Hard Riders president doesn't sound happy.

"We've got a situation. Black Dogs grabbed Sachs. Word on the street is Sachs stuck his nose into a drug deal and BD leadership took offense. Guess the Colombians also want in on the action in case Sachs overshares with the cops. BD's prez is still arguin' with the cartel leadership over what to do with Sachs, but we're not waitin' around for them to hold a vote."

"We know where he's being held?"

"Yeah," Hawke replies. "Fuckers have him in their clubhouse. Not tryin' to hide it, either—they're darin' us to come in there with guns blazin'."

"Trap?"

Hawke's mean-as-fuck smile broadcasts through the phone just fine. "'Cause they think if they shut down the Hard Riders, they get free access to East Las Vegas? They can try."

I'm pro-violence myself, but I'm also calculating the odds. I don't want to go in for Sachs and trade his life for that of another brother's.

Shit. Trade. I look at the pink RV. Fuck, I already hate myself, but it has to be done.

"We trade. We go after someone they care about and make a swap."

"You got an idea?"

"Evie Kent." We can trade Rocker—give him Evie, take back Sachs. Win-win for everyone involved.

"Not goin' to be a problem, you snatchin' Evie?" I love and respect my president, but the club comes first. Questioning my loyalty is for shit.

"Tell me to bring her in, and it's done."

"Do it," Hawke says. "The longer Sachs stays at the Black Dogs' clubhouse, the longer those Colombian fuckers have to mess with him."

Evie'll be safer at our clubhouse anyhow. I can protect her better there. It was stupid as shit to try for any kind of relationship with a woman like Evie. I'm not a repeat guy and we've had our fun.

Still, when Evie emerges from the RV, I discover the gratitude business is actually the other way around. Any thanking that gets done? It's gonna be me on my knees before her, because I'd be happy to drop and do some worshipping. Must be her version of biker chic, but she's wearing a pair of faded jeans that hug her ass. A blue-and-white T-shirt announces Happy Camper, which I certainly am because the thin cotton does nothing to disguise her red bra. Bright come-fuck-me red—my favorite color.

"Got a call." I need to tell her enough to get her to go with me willingly. "The Colombians are gunning for Rocker and there's a good chance they come after you since you matter to him. I'm seeing you back to your place. Or mine. Lady's choice."

"I'm not the one running drugs, so why target me?" Her fingers twist the edge of her shirt, and the gesture would be cute if she wasn't so naive. She's not part of the club and she runs a legitimate business for kids, for Christ's sake. Her life is as different from mine as a rabbit's is from a shark's. I'm the one swimming around all predatory and scaring the fuck out of people—she's the soft and fluffy vegetarian. But I've seen what the cartels do to make their point and now we have that road rage incident from the other day as Exhibit A. I'm not letting that kind of bad shit happen to her.

I pace her. Just keep walking, baby doll, and we don't have a problem. She looks at me as if I'm her Prince Charming and white knight extraordinaire. Which honestly makes me feel more like the horse's ass, because I'm not nice. More like I'm a founding member of Bastards Unlimited.

"Rocker's in deep." I fight the inexplicable urge to smooth the little crinkle between her eyebrows. I don't do comfort, either. All I have for Evie is a talented tongue, ten fingers and a dick I know what to do with. I shouldn't have started this with her. She's gonna hate me. Fuck. *I* hate me. "His club cut a deal and sounds like Rocker may have tried to up the ante."

She sucks in a breath. "What do you mean?"

"Rocker double-crossed the cartel, so they'll go after him any way they can—maybe put out a hit on you."

Her eyes widen and she makes a startled sound. Okay. So she really didn't know what her asshole brother has been up to. Either Rocker kept her in the dark or she refused to believe someone she loved could be that dumb. Problem is, she can't fix this for him and staying blind will only get her killed.

"Today sucks," she says softly.

"Sorry," I offer, meaning it. I'd like to fix her problems, although so far I'm coming up empty. Shooting Rocker only fixes *my* shit.

"If he's in trouble, I need to be there for him."

Appreciate her loyalty, but it's misplaced. Her brother is an asshole. When he turns up dead or worse, she'll hurt. Fuck that. Vik pulls up while I'm working through these unexpected thoughts. "You really want to get into this now? Because we both know I'm not part of your brother's fan club. Let me take you home. We'll figure something out."

She chews on her lower lip, thinking shit over. I've seen military campaigns conducted with less strategizing.

"Okay." She sighs and gestures toward the RV's passenger-side door. "Hop in."

# CHAPTER SIXTEEN

*Eve*

REV FIXES ME with a lethal stare. It's kind of cute—the man's more bark than bite.

"You want me to ride in a cage?"

Since he's the one who volunteered...yeah. "I have to get the Princess Mobile back to my place, and since I'm pretty certain flying and boating are out, that leaves driving."

There's a brief pause and then Rev holds out his hand. "Give me your keys."

"Do I look stupid?" I ignore him and head for the driver's side. He can ride with me or not, but I'm done. When I slide inside the RV and shove the keys into the ignition, however, Rev's right there beside me. He scoops his hands beneath my butt and lifts me off the seat.

"No cavemen allowed."

He grunts and drops me onto the passenger-side seat. "Out of your hands now, princess."

A guy who must be one of his friends strolls up.

He and Rev make arrangements for the other man to drive his bike back to his place and then we hit the road. Way too fast.

Rev drives the Princess Mobile the way he rides his bike. He's lightning quick, his gaze concentrated on the road as he takes each turn tight and hard. My poor vehicle hasn't exceeded twenty-five miles an hour in years, and he's pushing fifty. On city streets.

"Slow down. I can't afford a ticket."

"This thing doesn't go fast enough for a ticket." I silently point out the window at a speed limit sign and he grunts. "You think I can't afford to pay a ticket?"

"I don't want a ticket."

"Because you're such a good girl?"

"Because I have a strong personal preference for not breaking the law," I snap and roll my eyes. "I'm not unusual in that regard."

"Uh-huh." He brakes for a red light and slides me a sidelong look. "You gonna pout about my driving all the way home?"

I focus on the road. So I don't like breaking rules. I follow the law religiously. I don't even cheat the smallest bit on my taxes, which likely makes me the IRS's favorite small business owner. I've never written off so much as a single personal item. These are not character flaws.

Rev taps my knee. "Nothing to say?"

"I'm not in the mood to talk to you."

He hits the gas when the light changes. "Don't let me stop you, because I'm never gonna fucking live this down."

"You're the one who insisted on sitting in the driver's seat," I point out smugly. "This isn't my fault—and this isn't the way to my house. Do you need GPS?"

We're in an unfamiliar industrial area. Rev's sense of direction must suck.

"You need to know something," he says slowly.

You know what? I don't need to know whatever it is he's about to share. It's a safe bet it's designed to piss me off, and I've already achieved that state, thank you very much. In fact, I have a point I need to make very clear to Rev. Immediately. Do not pass Go, do not collect two hundred dollars.

"Pull over."

I'm tired of being the good girl. Of doing what I should, when I should. I reach over and grab Rev's dick through his jeans.

He freezes. "The fuck?"

I have to hand it to him—he doesn't crash us. He jerks the RV over to the side of the road.

I squeeze harder. "Now that I've got your attention, let's talk."

I'm not sure what happens next exactly, but Rev twists, my hand loses its grip and I fly backward. My head bounces against the seat as my back plants on the vinyl and Rev comes down over me, pinning me with his weight. My hands are trapped beneath me, which is my first clue that this teach-Rev-a-lesson scenario just derailed.

"I'm listening," he says slowly. "In fact, I'm in the mood to be perfectly fair. Tit for tat. You want my attention, it's all yours."

*Crap.*

"Think you made it a rule," he adds thoughtfully. "You do 30 percent of the chasing. I do the other 70. I owe you something now."

I should say *stop.*

I should stay mad.

Instead, just one word comes out of my mouth. "Please."

It's a stupid word and one I'll regret saying tomorrow, if not sooner. But I'm horny, I'm pissed off and I think there's something special between Rev and I, even if neither one of us knows how to talk about it. We both need more practice at this relationship thing.

His hand finds the waistband of my jeans. "You want this?"

"Please," I repeat, but this time it's more order than request. Screw asking him for what I want—I'll settle for telling.

He eases the jeans down to my ankles and then I step out of them. This shouldn't turn me on.

But it does.

Oh, God, does it turn me on.

My left leg brushes the seat; my right leg smacks into the dashboard. The lack of room is absolutely the only reason I hook my traitorous leg around Rev's ass. Truly, it is. I don't like him all that much right now. He's obnoxious, arrogant and way too demanding. No matter what we've done together, he's not in the driver seat of my life. I am.

Except I'm also spread wide on the front seat.

"Rev—"

"Shut up," he says calmly. "It's my turn."

I look down, as much as I can, and that's a huge mistake because heat rushes south. His hand disappears from view and then I feel his fingers stroking over the crotch of my panties. I yelp.

"You grabbed me." He sounds like the voice of reason. Given the way he's straddling me, I can feel his dick. Rev isn't a small man anywhere, as the long, thick part of him pressing against me attests. I wriggle, trying to free my hands, and he gets bigger.

I am such a lucky girl.

"We can't do this here." I'd like to say I protest because I'm sensible of where we are (parked by the side of a road). And maybe that factors in—but the real reason is logistical. There's not enough space to have sex here, no matter how badly I want it.

The pinning-me-down part is a little iffy, too. I've never tried tying a guy up or being tied up, and I should tell him to get the fuck off me. He'd do it. Rev promised me the first time he touched me that the games ended the minute I told him stop, so while I'd love to tell him he doesn't do it for me... I'd be lying. And with his fingers pressed against the crotch of my panties, he's gonna figure the truth out for himself anyhow.

"You're wet," he whispers roughly. "Even wetter than in the club."

He just had to bring that up. Yes. I'm that turned on. My panties are soaked, and if he moves his fingers, I'll come for him. The guys I've dated in the past have been foreplay guys. They've kissed and touched and run through bedroom tricks like they're working their way through a back issue of *Cosmopolitan*. And while I appreciated their efforts, none of them made me feel the way Rev does. It's like riding the orgasm Tilt-A-Whirl, one endless round of pleasure, when before I'd been standing all alone in line for the teacup ride.

He drags his fingers down my crotch and then tunnels beneath the lacy edge. Heat races through me as his fingers skim my slick folds, the pleasure so sharp and intense I swear I see stars. Or maybe that's just sunlight on a passing car. I don't know. I can't think, can't make my head figure out the logical thing to do. All I can do is feel.

"I could fuck you right here." His voice gets lower, rougher. Darker. I bet he gives brilliant phone sex. I buck and he pins me down.

"Tell me no, Evie, if this isn't what you want."

"Can't," I gasp out. I have no idea why he wants to talk now, when we could be doing other things. Kissing. Kissing would be good.

"Can." He gives me a dark smile and then shoves his fingers through my slick, swollen folds. Yes. I scream for him. God, I'd do anything he wanted right now. He penetrates me with two fingers, opening me up and pushing deep into my body.

"Ask me for it," he growls, twisting his fingers inside me and finding a magic spot. What should feel like an invasion feels so goddamned good. He works his fingers deeper as his thumb zeroes in on my clit. I collapse shamelessly beneath him, giving up any thought of resistance as my pussy tightens. Rev's shoulder strikes the steering wheel and he grunts.

"Let me up." We can drive to his place or mine. Find a motel. Something.

"Kinda like having you like this." He looks down, watching his hand, seeing me take his fingers and ride him. It turns me on, knowing he's so confident. He knows what he likes—and he's certain he can make me like it, too.

He penetrates me with three fingers this time, driving deep into my body. Not as if I put up any resistance. I'm swollen, wet for him, so slick that I can hear the wetness as he plays with me.

He brushes his mouth over my ear. "You still mad at me?"

This kind of discussion would guarantee world peace. Maybe our leaders should try it. I giggle at the thought and Rev nips my ear hard.

"Don't laugh at the man who's making you feel good." Warm amusement threads through his voice, though. That's something I'm figuring out about Rev. He doesn't judge in bed. Whatever works for me is his favorite thing, too. He finds my G-spot, his calloused fingers rubbing just right against a place that makes me see not just stars but an entire fucking galaxy.

My head shuts down, my body tight and focused on Rev. He's the center of the universe for me.

"Remember," he says roughly, as if he hasn't tattooed himself on every nerve ending in my body. "You started this."

"And you'd better finish it before I kill you." I finally manage to wriggle my hands free, but Rev is ready for me. He draws them over my head until my fingers close around the door handle.

"Don't let go," he orders.

I'm stretched tight, anticipation thrumming through me, as his thumb circles my clit and his fingers push slowly in and out.

"Or?"

"Or I'll stop." His laugh taunts me. "You want to end like this, Evie? Wet and tight, needing what I can give you?"

The man should have been a lawyer.

Not waiting for an answer, he moves down my body and I do my best to make room for him. He shoves my sopping panties to the side, his thumb still working my clit in lazy circles.

"You like me just fine," he announces, sounding way too fucking pleased. "This doesn't feel mad to me."

He works me with his tongue, tasting me, owning me. My panties vanish, along with all rational thought. Rev doesn't hesitate. He opens me up shamelessly, holding me in place with his hands on my hips. His mouth finds my clit, his tongue licking my slick folds as he pushes his thumb and fingers back inside me. I can't breathe, can't scream, and holding back isn't part of my plan. I hurtle toward my orgasm so fast that I yell loud enough to be heard on the street.

Pretty sure I scream his name. Might make more

than a few promises, too, my thighs squeezing his head, my fingers clenched around the handle. I'm pulled tight, stretched, and when the tension breaks, I'm all his.

# CHAPTER SEVENTEEN

*Rev*

EVIE IS FUCKING AMAZING. She moans and hollers, making rough, needy sounds that make me crazy for her. My dick wants to be inside her *now*, and never mind that we barely fit in the front seat of her ride. I want to shove myself deep inside her, so deep she'll never get rid of me. Mark her. Own her.

*Fuck.*

Evie demanded a relationship with her sex and I want to give her that, too. After the orgasms, the women at the club want to be paid or they want to talk. They want words, they want holding, or they plain want something I just don't have in me. As a result, I've dated my palm almost exclusively except for a few quick bangs when shit got too lonely or hard. Evie and I can't happen for real. She's my insurance plan for Rocker's good behavior. She's a marker I'm calling in.

She deserves more than a rough, quick finger bang in a car.

She deserves more than me.

Staring at the pussy I shouldn't tap, my fingers still buried in her sweet, slick body, I face the truth. I'm an asshole and I'm proud of it. She came hard, screaming my name as I rocked her world. Fuck the rules and what we should or shouldn't do.

I slide my fingers out of her pussy. For a second, she lies there, relaxed and open. Her T-shirt's pushed up above her tits and her panties are on the floor. Don't remember tearing them off, but I must have. Her pussy's the prettiest sight ever, pink and wet, the little hole begging for me to shove my dick inside her. Flip her over and get into her ass, too. No way I don't want to take her—and right now she'd let me.

I move back to the driver's seat. I'm in too deep here. "Nice show."

Kinda cute how she angry blushes. The pretty pink starts on her cheeks and it sure as shit extends everywhere I can see. She scrambles upright, shoving her shirt back down.

"You suck," she splutters, rummaging on the floor and coming up with her ruined panties. She looks at them for a minute but she's not a miracle worker. She drags her jeans on and shoves the scraps into her bag.

"And you came." I suck the taste of her from my fingers. Goddamned flavor of the month right there. Doesn't matter the expression on her face announces I'm the worst kind of pig. Doesn't matter because I know her dirty little secret.

She liked what I did.

She might not like me, but she likes my fingers and that's enough. She starts to say something, but I'm in no mood to hear it. I'm a complete fucking idiot because I can't keep my hands off her, and yet I'm handing her off to my club. What happened here will take on a whole new meaning, at least in her mind, when she understands the situation. I won't be her boyfriend, her down-low lover, her feel-good guy. I'll be the criminal who kidnapped her and made her face the unfortunate reality that her beloved baby brother is pond-sucking scum.

"You—"

I shut her up by sliding my palm over her mouth. Her teeth scrape my palm. "Bite me and I paddle your ass."

Fuck if she doesn't lick me. Christ. Heat tunnels straight to my dick, making thinking almost impossible.

"Whatever you start, I'll finish."

# CHAPTER EIGHTEEN

*Eve*

REV DROPS HIS hand and pulls the Princess Mobile back onto the road. That hand just did unspeakable things to me—and I loved it. He touched me and ate me out and now… Yeah. Now I have no clue what to do.

Bet Emily Post wouldn't have a clue, either.

I lean against the window in a daze, trying not to squeeze my thighs together. Holy crap. The man is out-of-this-world good. Little white-hot pulses of pleasure tease me as we drive and he knows it. The smug smile on his face makes me want to hit him. Okay, and then I want to shove him onto his back and ride him until he's the one seeing stars.

Huh. We seem to be taking the scenic route to my house.

We're in industrial central—and my neighborhood is row after row of matching houses with one palm tree and a small grass square in front and a concrete patio in the back. The only difference is the paint color and make of the car in the driveway. Rocker always jokes people will hit the wrong house when they come home drunk or tired.

These are not my streets, not my neighbors.

Granted, Rev has a penis. He's genetically incapable of asking Siri for directions or using the GPS, but he's been to my place before. He's no stranger to East Las Vegas. If he'd missed an exit or taken a wrong turn, I'd expect him to curse or to slow down. Instead, his face is cold and closed off, and the Princess Mobile is driving down the road at exactly the speed limit.

As if Rev really doesn't want to get pulled over or draw attention to himself right now.

Something's so wrong.

I fidget with my bag, working my phone out.

He doesn't take his eyes off the road. "Whatever you're thinking, just sit tight."

"This is not the way home." I punch the seat belt free and reach for the door handle. Yes, this is the stupidest choice I could make since jumping out of a moving vehicle at thirty-five miles an hour will hurt. A lot. But something's wrong here and I have an excellent imagination. I shove the door open and the road spools away beneath us, a lethal ribbon of hard, unyielding surface. I really don't want to do this—but I can't stay, either.

"Jesus." Rev curses and slams on the brakes.

I launch myself out of the RV, duck around the RV and run like hell.

A bike pulls up in front of me hard and Vik leans forward. "Princess doesn't get parole."

Oh. God.

I spin away from him, but Rev's out of the RV, stalking toward me.

*Rev*

This is what happens when I let my dick do the thinking.

Evie tasted so sweet that I forgot to remember what she is.

Insurance.

She bolted out of the RV like I'd held a gun to her head. She's pulling a runner on me and Vik's laughing his ass off. She ducks and weaves around the open car door, but Vik cuts her off easily.

"Hard way or the easy way?" I hold a hand out to her and her mouth opens. "Don't scream if you're voting easy."

There's a curse from behind her as Vik registers his opinion. He's not stupid, though. He doesn't touch what's mine. Because Evie is mine, even if she doesn't know it. Gonna make that clear real soon, along with a few other things.

"Fuck you," she breathes. That's not a scream, but then she turns and sprints away from me. Not sure where she thinks she's going because she's stuck between me and Vik. She tries to cut around the RV, feet flying. The fear radiating off her isn't unjustified because as much as I'd like to say I'm not planning on hunting her, I am.

I love hunting.

I count to three (I'm such a fucking gentleman) and then pound after her, not trying to hide my approach. Her feet scrabble for purchase as I lunge, fisting her T-shirt. Her ass hits my dick and I snake an arm around her waist, lifting her off her feet. No way she misses the hard-on poking her. Chasing her is a hell of a turn-on.

"You pig," she hisses. Pretty sure she's just mentally painted an X on my dick and plans on introducing her knee to that target.

"Sticks and stones, princess," I whisper against her ear and nip hard. I'd like to play with her until she's screaming for me, and not because she's hurting, either. "Are you still wet?"

She splutters incoherently, which will piss her off when she gets her head straight. Evie hates being out of control and not knowing what to say. I give her a few seconds to pull her shit together.

I toss her over my shoulder, immobilizing her kicking legs against my chest with one arm. Still, I take her point. She really doesn't like me right now. Fine. There's a long line of people who hate me—she can get in the fucking queue and take a number.

"Might want to be nice to me seeing as how I'm kidnapping you," I tell her.

She goes straight for the denial. "You can't do that."

I pat her ass. "Don't see how you can stop me."

Evie's learned something from our time together. She doesn't bother announcing her attentions—just opens her mouth and tries to scream. I flip her around, slap a palm over her pretty mouth, and adjust my grip so she can't bite. The neighborhood's shit, but somebody might notice.

"Stop playing," Vik says from behind me.

"Fucking love my job," I shoot back. "Don't rush me."

I nudge Evie's face up so I can see her eyes.

"We've got a problem, princess. Shit's happened between the clubs and that means you and me have a date at the Hard Rider clubhouse."

Fuck, that sounds dirty.

From the choking noise Evie makes, she agrees with me 100 percent, except I'm clearly the issue from her point of view.

"We're riding out of here. You can come with us, or you can fight. Gonna end up at my clubhouse either way, but I'll be in a better mood if you don't fight me on this."

She nods carefully and I lift my palm away from her mouth and set her back on her feet.

"I think you should go to hell," she says slowly. Vik snorts.

She tries to duck under my arm, as if that shit's gonna fly. I step closer, pinning her in place against the RV with my legs. She feels sweet as always.

"What's it gonna be, sweetheart?"

She goes wild, kicking and biting. Fuck, it's a good thing I'm wearing boots. Vik's laughing his ass off, the bastard. I grab her wrists and heft her over my shoulder. Her feet drum my ass, her mouth hovering perilously close to my dick and not because she wants to deliver my fantasy blowjob.

"Knock it off." I slap her on the ass, partly because I have a point to make and partly because goddamn she feels good. Love the soft give as my fingers mark her, putting my stamp on her skin. "Bite me and you kiss it better."

That stops her, although we both know she'll rally. Evie doesn't know how to quit for good. Hell, she probably still thinks I can be redeemed or saved or some shit. I adjust her weight so my shoulder's not digging into her stomach and open the passenger-side door. I drop her onto the seat and stare down at her.

I grip her chin in my hand and force her to look at me. "It would be a real bad idea to fight me right now. You might buy yourself a few minutes, but then I'd catch you again and I'd be pissed."

She opens her mouth, undoubtedly to argue. Her mistake is that she thinks I won't hurt her. I don't *want* to hurt her, but the MC comes first and I'll do what I have to do.

"Rocker fucked up. He took a brother and we want him back. You're gonna make sure that happens."

She licks her lips. "How do I do that?"

"Think of yourself as a bargaining chip."

"But—"

"Nuh-uh. The other option is that I shoot Rocker dearest the next time I see him."

Being Mr. Helpful, Vik pulls his gun out and thumbs the safety off. Evie stares at him, her panicked breathing coming way too quick as her gaze darts between the gun and me. If she hyperventilates, I'll have an even bigger problem on my hands.

"Come quietly and we'll save the bullets for later."

# CHAPTER NINETEEN

*Eve*

DEATH CHANGES EVERYTHING.

No one's dead yet, but Rev and his friend have made it plenty clear that the operative word is *yet*. No matter what my brother's done or not done, I'm not letting him get shot on my watch. I'm not entirely certain what just happened, but I think it goes something like this: I let Rev eat me out, he threatened to kidnap me, I ran, he caught me, and now we're driving somewhere I'm going to be really unhappy because kidnapping never works out as well as orgasms.

Also? My taste in men totally sucks.

I don't want to think about what I've let Rev do to me (or what I've done to him), so I focus on the basics. "Promise me something?"

He grunts and eases the Princess Mobile back out onto the road. He's entirely too comfortable committing felonies. I thought he was a decent guy underneath the rough exterior, but I've made my usual mistake, confusing a really talented penis with long-term rela-

tionship material. Okay. Lesson learned. If—when—
I get out of this, no more dating for the next seventy
years.

"Promised you you'd stay safe," he volunteers. "You
want something else?"

My wish list right now is impossibly long.

Yes, yes I want something.

"Promise me Rocker doesn't get hurt."

The words sound pathetic. I don't want to think
about how Rev's going to interpret them, but I'm more
than willing to beg. This is my brother, and he's in so
much trouble that my heart bleeds for him. And *that*,
ladies and gentlemen, is still better than what happens
when actual, real-life bullets start flying.

Rev shoots me an incredulous look. "Are you fucking kidding me?"

"No." I tuck my hands between my legs. "I'd really appreciate it if you promised me that my brother
doesn't get hurt. Whatever biker beat-down you think
you have planned for him, please don't."

He shakes his head. "You're incredible."

I don't think he means this in a good way, but I have
to keep trying. "He's my brother, I love him, and shooting would be murder."

"Don't have a problem with any of that," Rev mutters.

I believe him.

"But if you promise to keep him safe, I'll be quiet. I
won't tell anyone about—" I wave a hand. There really
ought to be a way to refer to your kidnapping politely.

"You'll come quietly?" Now Rev just sounds amused.

"Silent as the grave." *Bad choice of words.*

His curse doesn't say much for Rocker's chances. "I can maybe guarantee that the Hard Riders don't kick his ass too hard—because right now, sweetheart, I'll be honest and tell you that my president has a bullet with your brother's name on it—but I can't speak for the Colombians. He double-crossed them and they make me look like an angel."

"Just try?"

"Fuck." Rev's grip on the steering wheel tightens. "I'll do what I can, but I'm not a miracle worker. You need to accept the fact that your brother has pissed off a whole lot of people."

I can't be Rev's hostage or his insurance plan for Rocker's good behavior forever, which means I need a plan. The only thing I can think of, though, is that I still have my phone. As soon as I'm alone, I can warn Rocker and dial for help.

When we slow down, however, reality is waiting. Two big, ropey young men saunter forward when we pull up in front of a warehouse. Didn't know MCs came with valet parking. When I shift, looking around and trying to get my bearings, I can just make out the Strip, off on the horizon. When the sun finally sets, the whole sky will light up, but the artificial world of the casinos is so distant it might as well be on another planet. Not that the Strip isn't about money and power—it absolutely is—but the players there are less blunt about it.

"Is this the secret clubhouse?"

Rev grunts, which I decide is an affirmative.

Vik joins us and immediately passes a very familiar bag to Rev, who takes it and heads for a door about twenty feet away. Guess he figures I have no choice but to follow him. Well, fuck him and the Harley he road in on, because I'm not feeling real submissive right now.

Ergo, I stall. "You packed for me?"

Vik smiles slowly. "Had some time to kill and didn't think I was invited to the roadside party you were hosting earlier. Let me know if you're issuing rain checks."

My brain stutters to a complete and mortifying halt. Not only does Vik know what Rev and I just did, but he'd be happy to join us for some kind of kinky three-peat?

"Some bikers like sharing, baby girl." Vik whispers his next filthy suggestion against my ear as his big shoulders and body block out the rest of the world.

Catching up with Rev suddenly seems like the smarter plan. I hotfoot it over to where he waits by an industrial-strength door with a big metal grille.

"Don't fuck with her," he growls at Vik. The other biker flicks Rev a two-fingered salute and then saunters away. Rev shoves the key in the lock, opens the door and hesitates. Makes a girl wonder if he's hiding dead bodies in there because Rev is not a guy who hits the pause button on life often.

"It's not much."

"This is a kidnapping, not a five-star getaway."

"Uh-huh," he says and heads inside.

I'm not a Four Seasons gal. My finances won't
stretch to even a Motel 6, which means my vacation
options are limited. Rev's place turns out to be an
enormous loft. The walls are old brick and light pours
in from a trio of skylights high above the floor. Rev
could make a killing if he put this on the market—and
if having a biker MC as your neighbor wasn't considered a drawback.

Still, it's gorgeous. The light is awesome. And…

"I thought you said this was your place."

Rev shoves his keys into his pocket. "Problem?"

Absolutely. I have a long list, rank-ordered from
easiest to fix to outright impossibility. "Where's the
furniture?"

He shrugs. "Got a bed and a couch—what else do
I need?"

I snort and he swivels to stare at me.

"Classy," he mutters. I flash him the bird.

"Don't be fooled by the tiara." He's not kidding
about the lack of stuff. All I see is empty space. Rev's
place is one big room. I spot a small kitchenette at the
back and another door that looks like it leads to a bathroom. A circular metal staircase leads up to a loft. The
air smells like lemons and it's freakishly clean for a
guy. Maybe he has a service?

He glances around. "Kitchen's there. Bathroom's
on this floor—bedroom's up the stairs. Got clean towels in the bathroom. Not sure the sheets are as clean."

"I'm not staying. I have work."

"You're not going anywhere," he snaps.

"So we're having an extended slumber party, just like that?"

Because...no.

"You stay here," he repeats. "Take a break from the party gig for a few days."

"No." I can maybe miss a couple of events, but there's only so long my girls can cover for me.

"Like it better when you say yes," he says roughly. "Might want to work on that."

Rev hasn't hurt me yet, but I'd be stupid to trust him. Nothing about this situation is right. Kidnapping does not a dream date make. Sure I cut a deal with Rev that he'd let my brother leave without any bullet holes, but Rocker is free and clear for the moment and now I'm stuck here with a biker who is at best crazy and at worst homicidal. It's the story of my dating life—pretty on the outside and batshit crazy on the inside.

I need a plan, preferably a really good one. The bathroom door gives me the first inklings of an idea. Bolting won't get me far. Rev outweighs and outguns me, and I'm not desperate enough yet to hunt for a fire escape or a convenient window. Dropping from an upper-story window in a loft would kill me. My phone, however, is a lifeline.

"Permission to pee. Sir." I snap him a mock salute and gesture toward the bathroom.

Rev nods, so score one for me. Unfortunately, however, he falls into step beside me. Maybe he senses I'm up to something. Maybe he's got a thing for dirty kink, or maybe he just really doesn't have any personal boundaries. I throw out a hand at the door, slapping my palm against his chest.

"Personal space, big guy. You stay out here."

"The door stays open," he growls.

"I don't pee for an audience." Frankly, there's no way I could unclench with that kind of pressure. There's nothing sexy about using the bathroom in my book.

He curses. Worse, he actually has to *think it over*.

"You've got two minutes," he snaps. "And then I'm coming in after you."

Two minutes is better than nothing, so I nod and hightail it inside his bathroom, slamming the door behind me. It's spotlessly clean, but missing any kind of pictures, knickknacks or hand towels. It also lacks a window, which may explain his willingness to let me pee in private, and the lock is one of those stupid flimsy things set into the doorknob.

"Wouldn't bother with that lock." Rev's voice vibrates through the door. "It's been busted for months."

Shit.

I have one chance.

I slam up the toilet seat since he's clearly listening, and then I fish down my bra where I keep my phone and an emergency twenty-dollar bill. I message Rocker with shaking fingers.

ME: At Hard Riders clubhouse? Kidnapped by bikers. Need help ASAP.

ROCKER: Fck.

ME: Not kidding here.

I bring up the maps application, grab my address, and paste it into the text window. Rocker may know where the Hard Rider clubhouse is, but I'm not taking chances.

ROCKER: Gotcha

ME: Dialing 911 now

ROCKER: Hold that thought? Cops in club biz not a good idea. Sit tight and do what you're told.

ME: That's your plan?!

ROCKER: Cops can't help. Safest for me 2 if you stay quiet.

ME: 911 seems like better plan. Cops have guns and can help. Thought I taught you about Officer Friendly?

Rev slams a palm against the door. "Thirty seconds, princess."

ROCKER: I have their boy. We'll trade. Make it up to you later.

This is not a Pokemon card swap—this is my life. I glare down at my phone, torn. And what kind of life does Rocker lead that he's entirely unsurprised to learn

I've been taken hostage by a hostile biker gang? That he actually recommends I not call 911? And that he *kidnapped* a Hard Rider club member? I may not be a patch holder or own a bike, but I know a felony when I see one. I bring up my contacts, my fingers hovering over the 911 emergency contact info.

I should dial.

The bathroom door slams open. I back up as far as the too-small space will permit, but Rev's hard gaze narrows in on the phone in my hand. He moves so fast, I don't have time to flinch. His arms come around me, his hands twisting the phone out of mine as he drops the phone on the ground and rams his boot heel down on it, disconnecting my distress call.

"Get your ass in here, Vik," he hollers as I buck and twist against his hold. He kicks what's left of my phone out into the main room and then lifts me off my feet, bouncing me over his shoulder. The impact knocks the breath out of me—the man's shoulder is as hard as the rest of him—but I'm done playing by Rev's rules. I open my mouth and scream.

The front door flies open and Vik hurtles into the loft. He palms a gun as he comes toward us. Adrenaline pumps through me in a sickening rush. This is it. And because that pisses me off almost as much as it scares me, I scream louder. I'm not going out on a whimper.

"Fuck, she's loud." Vik stoops to collect the phone.

Rev slaps a hand over my mouth. I try biting him, kicking with my feet, but he simply shifts his palm to cover my mouth and my nose, cutting off my air supply.

"Fight me now and it won't end well for you," he growls. "You don't have to get hurt if you do what you're told. Nod your head."

Since I'm seeing spots, I nod. I'll recant later. Booted feet eat up the floor that spins nauseatingly beneath me. He removes his hand from my face, but doesn't slow down as he takes the stairs two at a time. I don't think Rev is an ax murderer, even if he is stupidly loyal to his MC, but this isn't the time to be taking anything on faith.

I open my mouth and Rev bounces me again.

"Really wouldn't do that," he says quietly. Despite hauling my ass up the stairs, he's not out of breath and unwelcome excitement pings through me. My libido has a horrible sense of timing.

He follows his warning with a slap to my butt that sends another tingle through me, the kind that homes in on my clit and reminds me that Rev has a dirty side. Vik shouts something about getting rid of my phone and then a door slams.

There's only one room at the top of the stairs, a wide-open loft with skylights in the twenty-foot ceiling. Spider-Man I'm not—I'm stuck unless I can get down the stairs. Rev drops me on the bed and stands over me, hands on his hips.

"We need to discuss the value of keeping your word."

"Or maybe you should look up the definition of *felony*."

This is crazy wrong, but a delicious shiver runs through me as he frowns. He's big and pissed off and I like this? Okay. I like him—and the only feelings he has for me are the wrong kind of possessive.

"We've got trust issues, princess."

"You think?"

"Yeah." He leans down, bracing his hands on either side of my shoulders. "See, now I don't trust you, and that means we're gonna do shit the hard way."

He drops onto the bed, swinging a leg over my hips. I squeak. It's embarrassing as hell, but the small, startled sound escapes from my mouth before I can bite it back. I blame it on the impressive bulge in his jeans now on eye level. He kneels over me, braceleting my wrists with his hands and drawing them up over my head.

Pinning me in place.

Is this another dirty game?

Why am I so stupidly conflicted?

"Rev?"

"Right here, princess." He reaches over and yanks open a drawer in the bedside table. Handcuffs. The man has handcuffs in his bedside table. Not like I was expecting him to keep the Bible there, but I'd have guessed porn. Maybe a paperback or a strip of condoms. I start wriggling in earnest because this is the opposite of safe. Those cuffs look like the real deal rather than a toy.

He tightens his grip on my hips and the bulge in his pants is definitely bigger than before. The cuffs click shut around my wrists.

Shit.

"Can we discuss this?"

"Time to do that, princess, was when we struck a deal that you'd come quietly."

For a moment I think he's done. Part of me is disappointed, but most of me is going for the gold in relieved. There's no relationship future when you end up tied to the bed without a safe word. I've coached girlfriends through shitty dates; I know how this goes. The minute Rev whipped out his shiny toys was the minute any chance we had together was over.

He stares down at me for a second, then curses.

"We're back to the trust issue," he informs me and then pulls a hunting knife out of his right boot. I shove away from him as far as the cuffs will let me go.

"Sorry, princess." He brings the knife down and I freeze. Can't even suck enough air in for a scream because no one can get here quick enough to rescue me. The blade slides between my bra and my T-shirt, the fabric parting far too easily. Cool air hits my bare skin. Shit. *Shit*.

"Don't scream," he repeats, his voice low and menacing. "No one's gonna hear—or care. You're my property now."

I squeeze my eyes shut. Okay. I'm a coward. I thought I knew Rev, but apparently I have no idea who he is or what he's capable of. He *told* me he wasn't a nice guy—and he didn't lie.

He peels my clothes from me, running his hands over the ruined fabric and coming up with my spare cash and keys.

The bed rustles as he shoves upright, then one big hand cups the side of my face. He brushes a kiss over the top of my head.

"Coulda kept your clothes on if you followed the rules. Might want to think about that, princess."

# CHAPTER TWENTY

*Rev*

THIS IS THE problem with hostage situations—they go FUBAR, leaving you holding the pieces. Evie's collateral damage and I don't like it. Hard Riders MC doesn't want to hurt her, but Sachs is ours and we've got a bigger problem in the form of the Colombian cartel anyhow. Hard to justify putting one person first—no matter how badly I want to fuck her. Nice to see the greater good bite me in the ass.

When Rocker finally calls me, I make him wait before I answer. "You know I'm not gonna talk to you about shit."

Guess his Colombian buddies haven't taught him any Spanish yet, because I understand every curse he aims my way.

"I want your word that Eve doesn't get hurt," he says.

There's a pause I don't try to fill. Let Rocker imagine what could happen to his sister while she's our "guest."

"You know I like her," I say finally. "She's a great girl."

"Promise me," he growls. "There's shit going on here that's out of my control. I can tell you that Sachs is safe enough for now, so make me the same guarantee about Eve."

"You don't want to demand I set her free immediately?" Have to admit, I'm kind of curious about that.

"The Colombians and I are not BFFs." He gives a grunt that might have been a laugh. "It's better she's not running around on her own."

"An eye for an eye. You know how I work." Even as I tell him this, I try to imagine hurting Evie. Epic fucking fail.

Another curse. "I hear you, but that's my sister. You hurt her, I hurt you back."

"While Sachs is with you, I keep Evie in my bed. Sooner you let him go, the sooner Evie can get on with her own life."

*Eve*

Being kidnapped is actually pretty fucking boring.

Turns out, I'm used to working and panicking about *not* working just doesn't fill enough time. Plus, Rev's underfurnished bachelor pad is not my idea of fun. The man could give Marie Kondo a run for her money in living minimalist because he owns no stuff. No books, no DVDs, no electronics. It's like he uses the place for sleeping, fucking and nothing else.

The one highlight? The handcuffs are back in his

bedside table. I woke up unlocked and I've stayed that way. I'd like to think if he tried tying me up again, he'd be in for a world of hurt. That I'd kick, punch and fight my way to freedom. It's hard to avoid reality, though. He's big, stronger, and he has a gun. If he wants to cuff me to the bed, he can.

When the door opens, I'm actually relieved.

Yes. I'm that bored.

Rev saunters in, carrying a plastic grocery bag. I'd like to ignore him and the delicious odors emanating from the bag. After all, I'm camped out on his couch because I'm desperate for a change of scenery. Downstairs, upstairs on the bed, or in the bathroom—those are my choices, and this is the safest one. I'm wearing a pair of yoga pants and a tiny pink tank top. Apparently when Vik packed for me, he either overlooked the bra drawer in my dresser or he couldn't be bothered, because there's not a bra in sight in my bag. I'm also barefoot because apparently shoes of any kind were also not on the packing list.

I bolt upright. "I have a job. You can't keep me here."

He walks right on past me and into the kitchen. The fridge door opens. Shuts. There's a faint clink as he twists off the top of a Budweiser. I'm not the neatest person in the world—I'm messy and I own it. But Rocker and his friends make me look like Martha fucking Stewart, as do my previous boyfriends. Rev likes things clean. And organized. I don't have to look to know that his bottle cap has gone straight into the trash.

He reemerges, bottle in hand, and sets the bag on the counter. "Dinner."

Great. I merit one word.

"How was your day, honey?" I blow him an exaggerated kiss, and score one for me, because his face darkens. "I missed work, thanks to a kidnapping asshole."

"Eating's optional," he growls.

How can he be so thoughtful and such a pig at the same time? And yes, I want to pick a fight with him. I'm missing work, Rocker's in trouble and something has to give. Surely Rev can't really keep me locked up here like some kind of medieval hostage. I'm aware that his MC is a law unto itself, but I do have friends—and that job. When you don't show up at a birthday party, the mom who was left in the lurch with her little darling sobbing her disappointed heart out will track you down and kill you. Plus, I have employees who like their paychecks. Eventually, someone's going to notice I'm gone.

"Nice to know you're not planning on starving me."

"I'm not fighting with you," he says slowly. "Fight's with Rocker."

"So explain to me what's up with *my brother*," I emphasize. "Tell me he's okay."

I've screwed up before and let Rocker down, but I've always had a choice about being there for him or not. This time, however, Rev's taken that choice away from me. Rocker needs me more than ever, and yet I'm not allowed to go to him?

"You always protect him?" Rev sounds amused, proving he's not as smart as I think he is.

"You think of your club brothers as family, right?" He drains half his beer. "Fucking straight."

"Rocker is my brother. I protect him. I look out for him."

Rev sets his bottle down. "You can't fix this for him, princess. He took Sachs."

"But kidnapping me won't make Rocker miraculously do what you want. It's just going to get you sent to the nearest correctional center for ten long years."

Rev shakes his head. "Keep thinking that all you want, but you might want to spend your time figuring out how to get through Rocker's head that he's lost. If he wants you back, he gives Sachs back."

"What if he doesn't?" I don't believe Rev would hurt me, but I'm not so sure about the rest of the Hard Rider club.

Rev gives me a hard look. "Let's hope it doesn't come to that, princess."

After dropping that little bombshell, he strolls up the stairs. A few minutes later, I hear water running.

Fresh out of plans and workable ideas, I try the front door. There's always the chance that Rev's gotten sloppy and left the thing unlocked with a getaway car parked out front. Hope's not a strategy, but it's all I've got.

The door's not locked, but when I open it, I discover two prospects standing outside. I flip them the bird and the closest one blows me an answering kiss. "Is that a suggestion, sunshine?"

"Fuck you," I snap. The kisser has a sense of humor worthy of a ten-year-old boy. He leans against the wall, shoulders shaking with laughter.

I march up the stairs and toward the bathroom.

And…hello.

Not only did Rev not lock the door, but he's whacking off in his shower. It's pretty damned impressive, and I don't mean the ink on his arms and down his back. I stand there for a moment, but there's just so much goddamned Rev to take in. The dick he's fisting is every bit as thick and long as I remember. The water cascades over him, droplets sliding down his chest and onto powerful thighs. His ass flexes as he hits some sweet spot and groans.

He raises his head and meets my glare. I don't know why I'm surprised, because Rev doesn't back down from anything. His club, his place, his rules. He thinks he's in charge of it all—and me.

"You want to have sex with me now, princess?"

Oh, fuck him.

He did not just say that.

Never mind that it's the truth—I know a power play when I hear one, which means I absolutely have to have the upper hand.

It's the principle of the thing.

*Rev*

Evie steps into the shower fully dressed and drops to her knees.

Jesus.

Not sure if I should cup my balls or say a prayer for my dick.

Narrowed eyes watch me from beneath thick lashes as she leans in and licks the tip. Holy. Fuck. Maybe that should be a prayer of thanksgiving I'm sending up because she owns me right now and we both know it. My body blocks most of the spray as I lean over her, bracing my hand against the slick tile, but she still gets plenty wet. Her top's fucking transparent in seconds, and given she's on her knees, she can see firsthand the effect her show has.

She's got gorgeous tits, the perfect handful with tight little nipples. Not sure why she's in here with me, but I'm enjoying my view. She licks again, her tongue rimming the head, and I bite back a curse. When she wraps her hand around my dick, I more than meet her halfway. Practically drill myself into her palm, but she just laughs. She's got a great laugh to go with those tits. Whole damned package is spectacular, but I can't let her control this moment.

"You gonna suck me or just admire the scenery?"

"You shouldn't be in such a rush." Her tongue makes another slow pass around my tip. Gonna fucking blow right there on her lips, mark her mouth and her face. Hit her tits, too.

She's beautiful.

Then she pulls back, and for a moment I think that's the whole point of our shower time. Makes sense she'd be out for a little revenge. She's gonna get to her feet and leave me standing here with my dick out and hard.

But then she licks her palms slowly and I almost blow on the spot.

"Dirty girl." Mean that as a compliment, too.

"Not sure I should agree with you," she answers and then wraps a hand around my dick and uses me as her very own slip-and-slide. Her free hand cups my tight balls, rolling and touching. Fucking show-and-tell as she sucks me into her mouth until I'm bumping the back of her throat and then somehow she takes that, too, making every wet dream I ever had come true.

And then she runs her tongue down my dick, her teeth lightly scraping sensitive skin, and there's only room for the two of us in this shower. She sucks and licks, and I'm fucking her mouth sweet and fast, watching her pretty pink lips form the dirtiest O around me. Don't know how she went from pissed off to this.

She drives me crazy, sucking harder and picking up her pace. Blow job's not a job and she knows it. Rough sounds tear from the back of my throat, filling up the space around us, and my hands fist her hair, guiding her down. I'm so close, so fucking ready to fill her mouth with my load.

"Fuck, princess." I tug her head gently. "Gotta warn you—"

She sucks me in deeper, and I lose the power of speech. She wraps her mouth around the head until her lips are bumping her fist with each hard thrust I make and I explode.

Bracing my hand against the wall, I force myself to stay upright. Holy. Fuck.

"You're goddamned amazing."

I pull her up into my arms so fast her head must swim, but when I'm with Evie I've only got the one speed. I'm balls-out and slow isn't happening. She reaches around me with a mean laugh that makes my dick twitch—fucker's already getting ready for round two—and kills the water. As if I care about that right now.

I carry her into my bedroom.

Kissing her like my life depends on it.

And maybe it fucking does, right? I head for the bed, ignoring her protests about water and the sheets. Evie worries too much. I yank the covers off the bed and set her down so quickly she bounces. Her arms and legs spread as she instinctively reacts to the free fall. Kinda like having her off balance for me, so I don't give her a chance to find her control. I fall, too.

I'd like to say I make this all about her, that it's her turn, and I've got plans to tease her for hours. Instead, I cover her body with mine. There's water everywhere, but she's slick and hot when I drag my dick between her pussy lips. So fucking ready for me.

"Rev." She moans my name, her fingers digging into my shoulder. I love the way she holds on to me, like I'm her anchor and she's about to fly apart.

Guess what happened in my shower was as good for her as it was for me, which just makes me harder. She needs me to give her this, and so I do. I always will. I roll on a condom and push myself into her. Don't stop until I'm all the way inside, her body hugging me as tight as her arms do. Her shriek almost fucking deafens me, and those sexy, happy noises she's making are definitely doing it for me, as well.

She just enjoys what I do to her. With her. In her. I pull back and then slide in faster, harder, drilling her into the bed. I know she likes her shit slow and sweet, but she drives me crazy and this is working for both of us. I love her hard and fast, arms braced on either side of her head because that way I can kiss her, touch her beautiful face, tangle myself up in her hair. She holds on tighter, her hips tilting up to meet my next downward thrust.

"Tell me you like this," I whisper into her ear.

Not like I can't tell, because her pussy clenches hard on my dick, doing some taking of its own, but I want the words. She moans something completely incoherent and so I pull back, give her just the tip. The next moan is a definite protest.

"Gotta give me the words, princess."

"I hate that name." She turns her head and fucking bites my ear. Hard.

She might not like the label, but I think she likes me. The way she comes is my first clue. And then, while she's still collapsed beneath me, I pull out and flip her over. Gonna hit her ass now. Not being a complete bastard, I lube my finger up good before I slip it inside it. She tenses up.

"Rev." My name's not a question, not a sigh, not a plea. Nope. She sounds nervous as hell.

"All of you, Evie. That's what I want." I ease my finger out, then push it back in, stretching her. Fuck, she's tight. Can't wait to get inside. "You want to tell me no, tell me now."

Evie sucks in a breath and squirms. Then she sighs. I fist her hair, pulling her head back until I meet her gaze. She doesn't say a thing, but she pushes her ass back against my hand. I give her a second finger, pushing deep as she inhales sharply, and then I scissor them open. Move slow and careful because I don't want to hurt her.

"I own this ass," I whisper against her ear. "You're mine."

"And you talk too much. Be gentle?"

"Yeah," I promise her.

I ease her up onto her knees, head braced on her arm. Goddamn, she's gorgeous like that, all trusting and open. I lube my dick because anything else would hurt her, and then I pull her cheeks apart and notch the head at the cute little pucker.

"Finger yourself," I order. When she hesitates, I cover her fingers with mine and we do it together. She's wet—I can hear it.

I thrust into her ass, slow and easy. Fuck, it feels good.

"Relax," I mutter. Reaching beneath her, I cover the fingers working her clit with my own. She deserves a reward for letting me have my way.

"Easy for you to say." Her words end on a gasp and a low moan as I seat myself inside her. God. Damn.

I fuck her ass sure and slow. Pull back until I almost pop out and then push back into her. When I go deeper, she gasps and bucks, but she takes me, her clit getting harder and fuller as we stroke together. She doesn't move from the position I put her in, either— just waits for me to move. Leaves me the illusion of control, because I can't hold back. I move faster and harder, rubbing her clit with the same rhythm until we're both gasping and reaching for the pleasure. Fucking find it, too. I come hard, filling her up, and she's right there with me.

I own her.

Mission accomplished. She's this biker's property.

# CHAPTER TWENTY-ONE

*Rev*

WAY TOO EARLY, my phone goes off somewhere near my head. Still naked, Eve's curled up against my side, her mouth pressed against my chest. Call had better be goddamned important.

"We've got company," Hawke says when I answer. "Think it's go time."

Hawke's the kind of man you follow because, wherever he's headed, it's either the right place to be or some special kind of hell that needs to be blown sky-high. I've done both with him. He's tall and rangy, dark ink covering both arms. A scar wraps around his neck like some kind of sick necklace—the most popular rumor is that someone (ex-wife, turncoat traitor, enemy soldier) tried to garrote him with his own dog tags. You can take two things as gospel. First, Hawke's hard to kill. Second, if you try to kill him, you'd better succeed or die in the attempt. Hawke doesn't do for-giveness—or second chances.

"Thank fuck." We've spent the last couple of days

hunting for Sachs and floating plans to pull him out of the Black Dogs clubhouse without losing any other brothers. None of us would hesitate to lay down our lives for him, but as Hawke points out, two-for-one is only an upside when you're stocking up on beer and chips.

If Rocker and his club were smart, they'd have handed Sachs over. Fuck, they wouldn't have touched him because starting a war between the clubs isn't in anyone's best interests. We've had a couple of tense, go-nowhere meetings discussing possible exchanges, but nothing concrete yet. Looks like things are finally changing.

"Twenty minutes," Hawke says.

"You planning on offering them tea and cookies?"

Hawke laughs. He's never been the nicest son of a bitch. "Thought I'd leave 'em at the front door. Let 'em think things over."

"Got a corner you can put them in," I volunteer. Beside me, Evie stirs and stretches. Waking her up is one more thing I can put on the Black Dogs' tab. I spread the fingers of my free hand over her belly.

"I assume you've got Evie close to hand," my president says drily.

I look down at my hand on her ass. Couldn't get much closer than that.

"She's right here."

"Get her ready," he says. "We'll make the swap and then we're in a better position to clean house."

"Promise me she's gonna be safe. I need to hear she's not walking into anything bad."

Hawke gives a bark of laughter. "Sounds like someone got too close."

Not too much I can say, since it's true.

"Rocker's her goddamned brother. He wants her back—you think he'd go to all this trouble just so he could hurt her?"

"I'm more worried about the rest of his club," I admit. "They could decide she's a liability and all this Colombian shit gives them a good cover story if they decide to make a move."

"You think they'd screw one of their own?"

"How do I know how they run their club? Seems clear they're not thinking straight, though, what with snatching Sachs and all."

"We make the trade," Hawke says. "If it looks like shit's headed south, we can step in. You want to go after her when Sachs is free and clear, that's your business and we'll have your back. You tell me if you're serious about her and we'll make it happen."

I've never thought about making a woman my old lady. Calling it a huge step is an understatement. I think about it for a moment, but we're under the gun here and I don't have the luxury of time. "Gotcha."

Hawke hangs up and I toss the phone onto the bedside table. Evie's still cuddled up next to me. She looks relaxed and soft, like a princess just waiting for me to wake her up with a kiss. Pretty sure I read a story like that once, but the reality's even sexier. I brush a kiss over her forehead and start moving lower. Not sure how Prince Charming stays hands-off because my dick has plenty of suggestions to make.

I plant a kiss on her shoulder. "We have to get up."

"Right now?" Evie's voice is warm and sleepy, her mouth grazing my chest. Another inch and she'd be tonguing my nipple.

Twenty minutes isn't much time. I've never had a problem getting up, putting my pants on and heading out the door, but this is Evie. As soon as I get her in my arms, I start thinking about staying. And yeah, banging the hell out of her because she's so damned sexy. She's also strong, which would make her a fucking amazing old lady. Not just because she's the hottest thing ever in bed (she totally is), but because she smiles when she sees me and she won't take my shit. Doesn't matter that I'm bigger, badder and could hurt her six ways to Sunday (not that I would, but she can't fucking know that, right?). She's still fighting for her asshole brother—and I'd like her to fight for *me* that way.

"Fucking love waking up next to you," I say roughly.

She sucks in a breath. "Not much for pretty words, are you?"

If she wants poetry, she's in bed with the wrong biker. I roll her onto her side, ease her leg forward and…shit. Can't take her bareback, no matter how much I want that. I grab a condom from the bedside table, roll it on and slip my fingers between her legs. She's warm and slick, but I need to hear her screaming my name so I press my thigh between hers. Glide my fingers over her soft lips, from her ass to her clit. It's like the world's best fucking happy trail. I could play with her all day.

"Rev?"

"Give me a minute." She's so soft, I could fucking come just grinding against her ass.

When I stroke my thumb over her clit, she moans and tenses up. She's wet, and that's good, but it's not enough. I cup her, pressing in with my fingertips, drawing slow circles on her slick flesh. Squeeze carefully.

"Come for me," I whisper.

She whimpers something. Doesn't sound like a *no*, so I stroke her some more. When I pinch her clit gently, she arches back into me, demanding more.

She can fucking have whatever she wants.

I roll a condom on and thrust inside her slowly. Don't stop until I've filled her up. And then I hang onto her hips, guiding her, letting her ride me as I move faster and faster, the two of us headed straight for the same goddamned wonderful place. *Perfect.* She clenches down hard, her fingers twisting in the sheets, and I drill into her one last time. Fuck, but she owns me.

I hold her tight, breathing hard. I've never felt like this, but I'm damned sure I want to do it again. And again. I look down at her, lying relaxed and boneless against me, and I'm pretty sure she feels the same way. Can't stop touching her, either. My fingers trace the soft undercurve of her spectacular tits, smooth down her belly, head south.

She wriggles away.

"Have to pee," she whispers, sounding a little tense. I can appreciate she's not used to sharing her space like this. We'll get used to it together. Not sure how to tell her what I'm feeling, but I'll figure it out.

I roll over onto my back, letting her go. By the time she gets back, I'll know exactly what to say to her. There's got to be a way to tell your woman that she's so perfect she's divine. And I'll find those words—in the ten minutes before our asses have to be downstairs and ready to roll—and somehow I'll get it right. Yeah. It's ridiculous, one of those long shots you see on TV when some world-class gymnast falls ass-first off the balance beam and is staring at those four inches. Knowing he has to get back up, get back on and kick ass. Somehow. With the whole goddamned world watching and armchair quarterbacking.

The bathroom door closes. I cover my face with my arm, because I'm happy living in the land of denial. Weather's awesome, scenery's great. This is absolutely all gonna work out. Evie brushes the side of the bed. Didn't hear the door open—woman moves like a ninja.

There's a soft, metallic click. Not a biker alive who doesn't know that sound of the handcuffs locking into place.

The fuck?

# CHAPTER TWENTY-TWO

*Rev*

I JACKKNIFE UPRIGHT as Evie scrambles away from the bed. Her foot catches in the sheets we kicked off—we've made a disaster of the bedroom—and she hits the floor. The landing doesn't stop her, though, because she pops back up and keeps moving until she's put the room between us.

Smart girl.

Takes a moment for me to focus though, which I blame on her. She's still naked and still so gorgeous I could look at her all night. Probably the rest of tomorrow and—because I won't shit myself about this—the rest of my life, too. I've already had this conversation with myself. She's got curves on her that demand a man appreciate them, curves that bear red marks on her skin from where my face scraped her. Fucking love seeing her wearing my mark.

She hesitates, the look on her face torn between elation and fear. Then she edges for the closet where her stuff is. Guess she's decided to pull a runner. I love her taking the initiative, but I need to shut this down.

She can't leave me.

I won't let her.

"You're into some kinky shit, sweetheart." I reach behind my head for the cuff, exploring the hinge with my fingers. She got it closed right, though, so I'm temporarily stuck. The key's across the room and although I could break the lock, right now I've got about ten minutes to see how this plays out.

"This isn't a game," she says softly. She yanks some clothes out of the closet and jerks them on. Shame to cover up such a pretty body.

"You think you can just walk out my front door?"

She shrugs. The motion sets her tits to jiggling, which is distracting. "Did you think I'd just let you keep me here? Do you really think I'm that naive?"

"Come back to bed." I pat the mattress beside my hip. "We can talk about shit."

I liked it better when she was cuddled up to me. I'd be happy to tell her that, or I could go for the show-and-tell. Way I see it, we fucked each other last night and it felt damned good. She let me in, and not just into her body. Christ, there's no way I let her walk away from me now. She's everything I didn't know I needed, and I may act dumb sometimes, but I appreciate her.

Fucking love her.

Huh.

Imagine that.

And since she's not a mind reader, I have to tell her. That part's gonna be awkward, but I have to do it. I'm not gonna risk losing her, and I sure as fuck want the whole world to know she belongs with me, same way I belong with her. Of course, the woman's hell-bent on putting some distance between us. She'll make it down the stairs, but I have prospects on the front door.

She hesitates. Don't think it's because she's missing me, although we'll work on that. Sure enough, she heads for the dresser. My gun's sitting on top, nice and visible.

"You want to shoot me?"

She glares at me. "Don't think I'm not tempted."

"Because personally, I think the sex was pretty damned good."

She ignores me, checking the gun to see if it's loaded. As if I'd carry an empty piece. I don't make threats—I make promises.

"Can I ask you something?" Shooting me will bring the MC running and the gun doesn't hold enough bullets to handle that kind of trouble.

"Let's trade," she says tightly. "You ask your question. I'll ask mine."

"Sounds like a deal, as long as you're not asking about club business. There's some shit I can't discuss with you. Club business stays club business."

"Believe me, I'm well aware of that," she snaps. She's definitely holding a grudge. "You've got thirty seconds to ask your question and then it's my turn."

Bet she doesn't realize it turns me on when she gets all bossy. It gives me ideas about showing her just who's the boss in our bed. But this is about more than just sex, no matter how hot she is. I need an answer to my question, which means I have to get the words out there. This isn't something I can force, and it's nothing I deserve.

"I'd like you to be my old lady."

She flinches, but I keep talking.

"Know that doesn't sound like every little girl's dream, but it means everything to me. Means we're a couple and we're in it for the long haul. You're mine. I'm yours. I'd be damned proud for the whole world to see you wearing my patch and to stand for you. I respect that you're pissed off right now, but this thing between Rocker and the Hard Riders is business."

"And kidnapping me was just business?" Her scowl doesn't look like a happy acceptance of my offer.

"You know how it works between the clubs. He disrespected us and he brought the cartel into our territory. We had to shut him down, and you were the quickest way to do that."

Her fingers tighten on the gun.

"Was the whole thing a set up? Were you ever interested in me at all?"

Since my *interest* is rock-hard and sticking out for her to see, I think she knows the answer to that.

"Why track me down? Why ask me out? Why follow me around? Do you fuck everyone who's related to guys you want to shut down?"

"I do what my president asks." That answer's not winning me any prizes, and sure as shit she flips me the bird. "But we're more than that. No matter what went down between you and my club, you're my woman. I've never claimed anyone before, and my brothers will respect that. You're different."

"So different you tied me to the bed," she mocks.

"Rocker's willing to trade Sachs for your safety." No point in not being blunt. "He's on his way over here to make the swap."

"Fuck," she says.

Yeah. That pretty much sums up our situation.

"Get your cute little ass over here and untie me." Part of it is a respect thing in front of my brothers—letting my girl handcuff me to the bed is the kind of shit that earns a man a new road name. No way I want to spend the rest of my life answering to Spanky or BD. Not the kind of moniker that inspires fear and respect in anyone. But most of it's that I just put my heart on the line for her. I asked her to be my old lady, to partner with me—and she hasn't answered.

Someone bangs on the door downstairs and Evie freezes.

"Out of time, sweetheart."

It's one thing to play sex games with her in our bed, but this is club business. The door opens—never should have fucking given my brothers a key—and boots thud on the floor. Vik bellows my name.

I give Evie a hard look. "Last chance."

She raises her chin and points the gun at me. Gotta give her full points for courage. "I'm walking out of here. Rocker's walking out of here."

The bedroom door busts open. Vik shoves his head in.

"Rev, get your ass out of bed."

Evie scampers over to my side, but then follows up the wise action with another stupid one. She raises the gun to the side of my head.

I gotta hand it to Vik. He keeps a straight face. I straighten up on the bed, trying to decide how to play this.

"See you're a little tied up," he deadpans.

I grunt something he decides to take as an affirmative.

His eyes take in the whole scene. Thank fuck Evie's dressed. "Didn't know you rolled like this."

"Shut up," I tell him.

"You gonna handle this? Hawke's getting impatient."

"Hey," Evie snaps. "I'm the one with the gun."

She sort of waves the gun around, which makes Vik briefly close his eyes. We need to go over a few basic safety rules, possibly after I paddle her butt.

"Handle it now," he growls at me. "Done waiting for you."

I'm done here, too. I tackle her, yanking her back against my body and twisting the wrist holding the gun. Hate doing it, but I can't let her keep threatening my brother. Plus, Vik's not the most patient guy—sooner rather than later, he'll disarm her himself and he won't be as careful. The gun hits the floor and I kick it away. I pin her against my side with one arm while she yells curses at me and I slam the cuff against the wall. Takes two tries for me to pop the hinge, but then I'm free.

Vik smirks. "Getting slow in your old age."

"Get the hell out of my bedroom."

Vik flashes me a salute and ambles out of the room. I shift my grip on Evie, who must realize that she's in a world of trouble here, because she's actually— briefly—silent.

"I'll give you some free advice. You pick up a gun, you keep it pointed in a safe direction."

The sound that comes out of her is more squeak than affirmative, but fuck this shit. I toss her over my shoulder, drag on my pants, shove the gun into my waistband and head downstairs. She fights me every inch of the way. Naturally. This would be way more fun if we were doing it naked in bed, but that's not happening now.

I smack her ass at the top of the stairs. "Keep it up and I'll drop you."

She screeches something highly uncomplimentary.

Our audience at the bottom of the stairs takes in the show. Nice to know my brothers are enjoying my pain. During the quick journey down the steps, I do a quick inventory. In addition to Rocker and two Black Dog brothers, Hawke and Vik crowd my living room.

"Put her down," Rocker snarls, starting toward us.

"You got Sachs hiding in your back pocket?"

Rocker snatches his phone out of said pocket and punches something in. "Pulling up in a cage now."

Hawke nods. "Put her down."

It sucks, but I do it. Evie flies straight into Rocker's arms. He tries to tuck her behind him, but she keeps hugging and patting him, like he's fucking five or something. She doesn't spare me another glance.

Hawke gives me a look. "You sure about this?"

"Make the trade," I tell him.

# CHAPTER TWENTY-THREE

*Rev*

ROCKER'S NOT THE dumb fuck I had him pegged for. After the Hard Riders trade Evie for Sachs, he moves into Evie's house. I know this because I still keep an eye on her. He also keeps a couple of prospects nearby, so either he's wised up and decided she needs a body-guard, or he knows there's a credible threat. Not sure which pisses me off more.

I pull up behind her house two weeks after the trade. It took four days to find the right guy for this job, which is two days longer than I expected. The Feds never believe that most of the MCs are on the up-and-up, so they always have their plants. I trust my brothers and the prospects are vouched for, but that leaves the hang-arounds and wannabes. There are always guys looking to join, who show up at the clubhouse and on runs, buying rounds and looking for an in. That's where the Feds like to place their boys. If one guy doesn't move up in the club hierarchy, they just send in another and another. I'd done some looking and some talking, and it turns out Benjy had joined us just three months ago. He had a big, shiny-ass bike and way too many questions for a guy looking to patch in.

*Hello, plant.*

Hawke and the club leadership discussed it. Doesn't sit right, bringing in the Feds, but it's the cleanest solution. Rocker is the connection between the Black Dogs and the cartel; Sachs confirmed as much.

Sachs made the call from a burner phone and wouldn't you know—Benjy's all over that intel like a dog with a stick. Couldn't drag him away from Rocker after that, which solves two problems. Gets him out of our club and sets Rocker up for the fall. Whatever happens now, it takes Rocker out of the picture. Even if he doesn't talk when they bring him in, the cartel is gonna suspect he did. They'll throttle back on their operation, too, waiting to see if the feds have made them, too. It buys the Hard Riders time to come up with a permanent solution.

We've gone over the plan a dozen times and now it's out of our hands. I wonder if Hawke's planning any side action. Now's the time to hit the Black Dogs. After Rocker goes down, they'll be reeling and looking for the sneak who sold them out. Damned glad I'm not Benjy, but I'm betting he's got an escape plan in place. We're uneasy allies in the war on drugs, but I don't want to see him get plugged. We're fighting on the same side—just with different weapons. Still, feels safer to go in myself. This outsourcing shit isn't my thing. Can't control the outcome the way I can when it's my finger on the trigger.

Rocker pulls up in a white van, Evie right behind him in her pink RV. He's been glued to her side since he brought her out of the Hard Rider clubhouse. She parks, but for a minute I think Rocker's not gonna stop. The van idles, but he doesn't kill the engine. Evie pops out of the RV, smiling and laughing. Christ, she looks good. She heads for Rocker's van, her skirts all sparkly and shit in the sunshine, and I'll bet he's cursing up a storm.

He kills the engine—and all hell breaks loose.

Local authorities bring out the SWAT team for anything involving gangs and guns. They must have a warrant to go with their suspicions and Benjy's intel. Not like they pop out of fucking nowhere, but it feels like it. One minute, the street's empty and the next it's full of SUVs and there's a BearCat driving down the center of the road. Doors fly open and there are suddenly about twenty police officers in black vests marked POLICE swarming all over Rocker's ride. And then the SWAT team members in full camo and Kevlar. Not like I like seeing a bunch of M-16s pointed at my girl. Nothing I can do from here but pray, and I'm damned rusty at that.

Evie screams and she's surrounded, rushed to the sidelines. The cops bark out orders and Rocker emerges from the van, hands up.

He rakes the boys in blue with a smile. "One fuck of a welcome home committee."

Those cops put him on the ground way harder than necessary and pat him down. Doesn't take them long to find his piece tucked in the small of his back. That's almost all they find, though. Rocker's got a couple of illegal semiautomatics in the back of the van, but he's drug-free.

Weed makes for a bulky cargo. It takes a hell of a lot of product to make good money, and it stinks like crazy if you don't package it right. There's not a drug dog alive that won't tear you and your ride apart to get at it and the customers who buy that shit aren't loyal. They're not addicts and most of them have lives they'd like to keep. If they get busted, they sing. Plus, if you get busted while carrying a gun, the penalties get stiffer. Rocker's Colombian connections are pushing harder stuff than that and the man's a pro. He does exactly what he's told. No resistance, no extra words. Just tells them he pleads the fifth and wants a lawyer.

They won't get him for drugs, but the weapons charge will stick. The dogs find nothing in the van, but it's merry fucking Christmas when the cops go in. Not like the back is full of coke or guns, but the fact that Rocker's transporting a pair of semiautomatics is enough in the hands of a zealous prosecutor. They know he's dealing, even if they can't prove it, and they'll use the guns as an excuse to put him away.

I watch, Vik by my side. When the cop cars pull away with Evie and Rocker, I fire off a quick message to Hawke from a burner phone. There's no point in being stupid about this.

ME: Rocker busted. Feds all over him, but no drugs. Dumbass was transporting guns, so he's not walking. Worried that they took Evie in too.

HAWKE: Got a lawyer on it. If your girl's clean, it's a bad couple of hours and then done.

ME: Gonna head down and meet the lawyer. Wanna be there when she gets out.

HAWKE: Your call. You show, she gonna suspect?

ME: Not stupid

HAWKE: So that's a yes

ME: Thinking so

HAWKE: Bring a big fucking bunch of flowers

Shoving the phone back into my pocket, I nod to Vik. "Let's ride."

He sighs dramatically. "Are we playing white knight? You about to ride to the rescue?"

I flip him the bird and peel away from the curb. He's right behind me all the way to the police station. When I get there, the club's lawyer is just pulling up in his fancy-ass Mercedes. James Brandon didn't waste any time getting here and I appreciate that. Lawyer Boy's not bad-looking, which probably helps with the jury, and he's wearing a real slick suit.

"Mr. Brady." He tips his head at me. Then he strides into the station. I follow right on his ass. He gives me a look, but doesn't say anything. When the front desk asks his business, he announces he's representing Eve Kent and they wave him through.

I'm more of a problem. We're not married. I'm not her brother, her family, or her legal representation.

James earns his goddamned paycheck. "He's Ms. Kent's fiancé."

This white lie earns me a seat in the waiting room. It's not the happiest place on the earth, so I'm ready to go when James texts me an hour later that we're good to go. I head out to meet them. Evie's gonna need a ride home.

# CHAPTER TWENTY-FOUR

*Eve*

NO ONE PRESSES CHARGES. Even though I've done absolutely nothing illegal, this still feels downright miraculous. Better yet, my mistaken arrest didn't happen at a party, so I may be safe business-wise. I want to belt out "Miracle of Miracles" and get my inner *Fiddler on the Roof* on. Except this particular problem is just the tip of the iceberg, isn't it? Rocker's not striding down the hall next to me and the lawyer Rev provided—he's still locked up somewhere.

There has to be something I can do. "When does my brother get out?"

James hesitates so briefly that I almost don't catch it. "Mr. Kent has different legal representation."

"But surely his lawyer can get him bail?"

"I'm not sure if the judge will refuse to set bail or not. In forty-eight to seventy-two hours, the District Attorney will bring charges against him at a hearing. You'll know then."

*You.* Not *we.*

I'm about to press for more details when I spot Rev
leaning against the wall, waiting for me. I don't know
what to say or do—I'm pretty sure today is out of
miracles and Rev scares the hell out of me at the same
time he comforts me. Right now I don't know how to
work with that.

Rev shoves his hand in my direction. "Let me take
you home."

I'm too tired to protest. We head outside. There's
a brief problem when I realize that riding behind him
on his bike in my princess costume is a challenge. We
work it out, though, bunching up the fabric between
us. It looks ridiculous, but I'm beyond caring. I manage to hold out most of the ride without talking or crying, but then I fold.

"I can't do this," I tell his back.

"Why not?" he asks.

"You ride to my rescue, but maybe I wouldn't need
the rescue if you weren't..."

"If I weren't what?" His voice is tense.

I wish I had an answer to that question. Rev's been
good to me. I can't deny it. He ponied up a lawyer
and I'll bet he had bail money ready, too. He'd promised to have my back and he did. Problem is, things
happen around him. Illegal, rule-breaking, stressful-
as-shit things.

He looks around at me. "Is this about Rocker getting arrested?"

Rev's plenty of things, but stupid isn't one of them.

"Are you telling me you had nothing to do with
that?"

His grip on the bike tightens. "Thought you'd prefer that to the alternative. Usually, when I take care of a problem, the solution's more permanent."

That kind of problem-solving approach is why we can't be together. I use my words—he uses his gun.

He curses loud enough to be heard over the bike's engine. "Just tell me what you want."

"I don't know." Honestly, there are so many competing wants and needs in my head that by rights I should explode. Rocker walking out of that jail a free man tops the list, however. I'd like him to head off to a glorious future complete with gainful employment, a college degree and a two-story house with a swimming pool. I'd like to know that even if he doesn't achieve those things, he'll be happy with whatever he does decide to do. Given the minimum sentencing requirements in the fine state of Nevada, however, all of those plans will be on hold for at least five years.

Way too quickly, Rev pulls into my driveway. It's not a quiet entrance, thanks to the bike. Plus, the entire neighborhood seems to have a pressing need to take out their trash—and they're taking their sweet time, eyes fixed on me and Rev. And since their last sight of me was in the back seat of a cop car, getting carted downtown, I can imagine all too easily what they're thinking.

Samantha comes rushing out to wrap me in an embrace. "Are you okay?"

The short answer? No. No, I'm not. I've been arrested. Rocker's gone and it's unlikely he's coming back. I've talked to more law enforcement today than

I have in my entire life, and I now have a lawyer of my very own. The long answer is still no, but comes with a hundred-point, itemized bullet list of everything that's gone wrong with my life in the last twenty-four hours.

I pick the most obvious problem. "Rocker got arrested."

Samantha sighs. "Yeah. I heard about that."

"I think he's in trouble for real this time."

Samantha gives me a *no shit* look that urges my sorry ass to move out of the land of denial, stat. Rocker's *definitely* in trouble, the kind of trouble accompanied by a six-figure bail bond and an urgent, pressing need to find the very best of lawyers.

The neighbors' stares bore into me, and it's far too like that last time I left Rocker and came home to find him sitting on the couch with Officer Friendly making plans to take him away from me. I should have done something different, done something more. There had to have been some way to fix this before things ended with Rocker in jail and me accepting legal advice from a lawyer working on retainer for a motorcycle club.

Bottom line?

I failed Rocker.

Again.

Rev stands behind me, his hand on the small of my back. It's actually quite nice and supportive. Downright polite and civilized, except that I can feel every inch of that touch burning through my dress, making me want to drag him inside and lose myself in him.

Hot sex followed by a side of orgasm-induced oblivion is tempting, but I've already tried it.

It hasn't worked out well for me.

*Rev*

Evie gives me a death glare. "This has been the worst summer ever." And then she fucking smacks me in the middle of my chest. Hard. "I blame you."

I'll take the blame up to a certain point. "Rocker came up with his shit drug-running plan all on his own."

Her face sort of crumbles and she chews on her lower lip, blinking her eyes like crazy. Screw the plan to stay away from her—I pull her into my arms, ignoring Samantha.

"Sorry, babe," I whisper against her hair. I am, too. I'd like to kill whoever approached Rocker and talked him into dealing. I either break shit on purpose or I fix it. That's how I'm wired. My old man was in the business of fixing people's souls, but I'm more practical.

"Promise me you'll help him," she orders.

I run my hand down her back. Avoid her ass, too, because I'm a gentleman like that. "You gotta learn to ask nicely."

"Maybe you need to learn to do what you're told."

Yeah. Not a fucking chance of that.

"I do requests," I offer.

"This is why we'd never work out." She sighs.

"Not disagreeing with you." I ignore the unfamiliar stab of something at her casual dismissal of an *us*.

She's not wrong, and hooking up with my hostage is downright stupid.

We stand there for way too fucking long. The Colombians could swing by and make a house call and there we'd be. Standing in plain sight. Might as well paint a target on our chests now. Not bad here, though, holding my girl. Evie's soft and warm against my chest as she leans into me. Parts of her trust me, at least when she's not talking.

"Please," she says finally, although she says the words to my shirt and not to my face. Guess she needs some practice, too.

"It's club business."

"You guys are crazy," she announces and I can't disagree with her. When you ride with the club, you live by a different set of rules. In my world, you figure out who made shit explode and then you go after them. If the cartel came into our territory and stirred shit up, we'll hit them back hard. Otherwise, they'll keep pushing and taking until there's nothing left.

She hates my club. To be fair, I think all MCs are on her shit list at the moment, with the Black Dogs sitting at the top. She doesn't understand what makes a bunch of men decide to ride together, to band together and pledge their lives to one another and a largely unwritten set of rules. We're family the same way she and Rocker are, and I've just put my family first at the expense of hers. I rub my hand up and down her back, but there's no way to fix this now. The only way to right the wrong I've done her would be to magic her dumbass brother out of jail and back into her life.

I'd like to tell you I'd do it, too. That I'd give her whatever she wants, when she wants it. In bed, that's true. Hell, pretty much any other time it would be true. But this thing with Rocker is bigger than both of us.

I'd like to give him back to her, but I can't.

He's a fucking menace who runs arms and sells drugs, and I can't let him do that anymore. And don't tell me it's not my job to stop him. I may not be an FBI agent, a cop, or a member of the goddamned SWAT team, but I have a responsibility to say something when I see shit that's not right. You ever see those signs in the airport? "See something, say something"? That applies here, too, and Evie knows it—she's just not ready to admit it yet.

And so no matter what I tell her, no matter how nicely I rub her back and promise her that everything's going to be okay and I'll do what I can to help the dumbass, we both know it's not entirely true. At some point, I'm going to let him hang himself with the noose he made. I wouldn't bring him back even if I could, because then he'd just do it all over again.

And that's not right.

Think she's got that figured out finally, because she steps away from me and grabs Samantha's hand. "Thanks for the ride."

She's dismissing me.

I grunt something as she heads inside, but fuck if my feet don't move. It's like they're permanently planted in Evie's driveway, watching her walk away from me. I get that she doesn't trust me.

Hell, I wouldn't trust me, either.

# CHAPTER TWENTY-FIVE

*Eve*

EVERY KID DESERVES the birthday party of his or her dreams. I've brought some weird requests to life—kids ask for the strangest things and then enjoy the shit out of them. There's no point in not going for what you want—or in letting other people make you feel weird or bad for your own personal preferences.

Rev's like that in bed, although I'd rather not think about his prowess in the context of kids. That's just creepy.

After I left him standing on my driveway like the ending of a bad, sad movie, I went inside and did some thinking. Lots of thinking—it was days before I came to any conclusions. I found Rocker a lawyer. I learned that the district attorney considered him a major flight risk and bail had been denied. I visited, which was thirty minutes of awkward on my part followed by fifteen minutes with a box of tissues afterward. I hope he's going to be okay. We all make choices every day, and I still want nothing but the best for him. His recent choices, however, have been the wrong ones and they come with a price tag.

In a few years, I hope he can make new, better choices. I hope he finds a new beginning and a new life, even if the old one is now on hold. Forgiveness. Atonement. Redemption. Pick a noun. I wish all of those for Rocker. Today, however, I'm making a choice for myself.

The day's sunny, the weather perfect for BBQ and beer. The bikers aren't my usual crowd, but a few kids run around the bikes like sugar-fueled maniacs. Mary Jane brought hers and Tío gives me a head nod from across the courtyard.

When I called Vik, I thought he was going to have a stroke. You remember the offer he made me the last time I was here? About bikers sharing? Yeah. I told him I wanted to take him up on it. He almost hung up on me, which was both cute and inconvenient. Not that he's opposed to a threesome in bed, but he's decided I belonged to Rev and my pussy has a no-poaching sign on it.

I straightened him out.

I want to share Rev with the Hard Riders MC.

Which is why I'm here now. It's Rev's birthday today, according to the driver's license he flashed in my direction the day I met him.

Vik slides me a glance. "You sure about this?"

Nope. Not at all. But I want my man back. I want the guy who discusses favorite colors with a five-year-old girl, who eats cupcakes and takes me for rides in the desert and who believes oral sex is the answer to every argument. He's not a nice guy, but he's mine and I need him in a way I've never needed anyone before. And if he's a biker who comes with a bunch of rough, loud, filterless bikers, I'll love that part of him, too, because *they* love him and they're his family.

Rev tears into the courtyard, going too fast as always, and then he brings the bike to a fast stop. Does some staring.

We redecorated when he rode out this morning. The Princess Mobile is parked on one side of the courtyard with enough balloons to float the thing into outer space. We've got cake and beer, and yes, we have fairy wings. I tried to convince the club to jump out and yell "surprise," but Vik said that would get us all shot and then he and Hawke started arguing about how many guys would get plugged if Rev was startled.

Rev straddles his bike, silently taking in the scene, but it's a good sign he doesn't point his bike toward the exit and leave. His gaze moves down my body, taking in my outfit.

What there is of it.

Since this is a biker princess party, I've made a few modifications. My dress is still pink and sparkly, but it now stops mere inches south of my butt. I'm wearing black motorcycle boots (with pink laces) and a leather vest I borrowed from Vik. It doesn't have any patches on it, but I improvised and embroidered Happy Birthday on the back. It's silly, it's fun, and…

I have no idea how Rev will react.

Maybe…

"Happy birthday." I walk up to him, still watching

his face closely. Then I lean in and put my hands on his thighs as I brush a kiss over his cheek.

Oh my God. What if he lied about his birthday on his license? What if today *isn't* his day?

He looks me over. "That's one hell of an outfit."

"Dress for success, right?" I pivot slowly so he can get the full effect. He must like it because he lifts me up onto the bike in front of him. There's not a hell of a lot of room, so I end up facing him, my legs wrapped around his hips.

"Hey." He drops his forehead to mine.

"I missed you."

Please let that be enough.

He's quiet for a moment. "Is that all you have to say to me?"

"You want me to sing to you? I do a mean rendition of 'Happy Birthday.'"

"I want to know where we're at." His thumb teases the corner of my mouth.

"Truth?"

"Always."

"I want to choose you. I want you to be in my life, both when I get up in the morning and when I go to bed at night. I want to wake up with you and fuck with you and do a whole lot of loving and living together. I want us to ride and then come home and do whatever it is that couples do when they're not fighting or having makeup sex. I want us to figure it out together, and I want you to be happy."

He pulls me closer, so close that I'm straddling his dick. His dick's ready to kiss and make up, or maybe that's because I wriggle a little, just in the interest of getting comfortable.

"Makeup sex?" His mouth brushes my ear.

*Please.*

"I want another chance at us."

He wraps his arms around me. "That it?"

There's one thing I haven't told Rev yet, and I need to do it before I chicken out. "No. I love you. I know you don't do relationships and I'm pretty damned rusty at them. I overplan and overthink, and I've never met a rule I didn't like, while you're more of a saddle-up-and-ride guy. I have a plan and you have a mission, and we're bound to fight. But... I love you and everything else is just a detail."

Rev's hands slip beneath my short skirt and cup my butt.

"So I'd like you to tell me if you're willing to give us another shot. Tell me what you need to make this happen, and I'll figure it out."

Rev stares me. He looks a little stunned.

"You love me."

"I do."

See? That wasn't so hard to say.

And then he makes me wait. He stares, his mouth dipping to my mouth and lower. His fingers tighten on my butt, and time sort of stretches out and out and out.

God, he's killing me.

"You made me a promise."

"Uh-huh. Said all sorts of things." He buries his face in my neck.

"You promised I'd be safe with you, that I'd never be hurt again. And then you made me an offer."

I'm stretching the truth a little, but it's in a good cause.

He raises his head, frowning. "Who the fuck hurt you?"

"You can."

His frown gets deeper.

"Better tell me how, because I promise you I'll never fucking do it again."

"I want us to stay together and I want to be your old lady. You promised to keep me safe, and I'd like to think that means my heart, too."

I study his face anxiously, because maybe he's changed his mind, or maybe he didn't mean it at all. I've thought of a thousand different *maybe*s since I walked away from him.

"Fuck yeah," he growls. "I love you."

*Rev*

No fucking trumpets. No bells, no fireworks, no sign in the heavens. I pour out my heart to Evie and she stares at me, wiggling nervously on my lap. Don't think she knows what she's doing to me, but she's gonna find out soon. My dick's already skipped ahead to our happy ending.

"Gotta get a couple of things straight, though." I appreciate her coming here and the birthday party's cute, but we haven't done enough talking recently.

"Okay," she says, more slowly this time.

"We good when it comes to Rocker?" Her brother's looking at some serious time, and we both know I had a hand in it. If he gets his act together, I'll wish him the best, but he's currently out of choices.

She slides her arms around my waist. "Wish things could have gone differently, but…yeah. We're okay."

I make a note to get the club's lawyer on Rocker's case. Maybe there's some way to make things easier. Worth looking into.

"And you understand that this thing between us is long-term?"

She nods.

"Then we're straight. Didn't think I'd get a princess out of it."

She grins up at me. "No more princesses."

"Huh. I kind of liked it."

"I'm upgrading." She gives me a determined look. Probably should be getting nervous right now, but this is Evie. She gets whatever she wants. "I'm planning on being the queen of your heart—the same way you're king of mine."

"Uh-huh." I almost keep a straight face, but then I bust out laughing. She slaps at my chest, but she's giggling, too. "Fucking corniest line I've ever heard, sweetheart."

I pull her close, kissing her cheek and making for her mouth. Probably should stop there since we're sitting on my bike in full view of my club. "Love you anyhow. Can't believe you're choosing me."

"Always," she whispers. "As long as you want me."

Not gonna have a problem there.

That's one fucking promise I can make. "Forever. You and me."

* * * * *

*Read on for the next book in
Anne Marsh's* HARD RIDER MC *miniseries,
INKED.*

# CHAPTER ONE

*Vik*

Before I touch even so much as an inch of sweet, creamy skin I know I want to mark her. Make her mine. Doesn't hurt that she's wearing plain white cotton panties, the kind designed to cover up rather than to showcase. But that makes a man like me think about turning good girls bad. She's tucked the waistband down to give me more room to work. Thoughtful, right? I can't stop looking at the tattoo chair where she's spread out, waiting for me to ink her. I'll be her first because nothing but virgin skin meets my greedy eye.

I grab my sketch pad from my rolling table. "You got a design in mind?"

She shrugs and her blouse rides up her spine. "Not yet."

"You trust me?"

"Absolutely not," she says, proving she's as smart as she looks. "Tell me what you're thinking."

"Firebird." I drag the Sharpie over her skin, bringing to life the image I see in my head. Maybe she won't appreciate wearing a Russian fairy tale on her skin for the rest of her life, but she's not exactly timid and the bold black, orange and red lines tracing the equally strong lines of her back feel right.

"Firebird's a thief and hard to catch. She almost gets busted stealing the king's apples when the king sets his sons to catch whoever's been trespassing on his shit. Ivan gets a hand on her, but all he's left with is a single fucking feather. She leaves and he spends fucking forever chasing after her."

"Okay."

I embrace the familiar adrenaline rush as I draw, sketching the outline of a bird, wings outstretched as she takes flight. To freedom. Her tail curls down, teasing, flirting, broadcasting a fuck you to the man she leaves behind her in the orchard of the king. This is my skin, my piece of her to ink, to own, to give back to her filled up with the story she's shared with me. Right now, I own her and she's mine. She relaxes into my touch, my calloused fingers scraping gently, carefully over her skin, preparing her. Fuck playing by the rules.

I grab my needle and brush my mouth over her ear. "This is gonna hurt so good."

\* \* \* \* \*

# LET'S TALK
## *Romance*

For exclusive extracts, competitions
and special offers, find us online:

Or get in touch on 0844 844 1351*

For all the latest titles coming soon, visit
millsandboon.co.uk/nextmonth

*Calls cost 7p per minute plus your phone company's price per minute access charge